ALSO BY KD ROBICHAUX

THE BLOGGER DIARIES TRILOGY
Wished for You

Wish He Was You

Wish Come True

THE CLUB ALIAS SERIES
Confession Duet (Before the Lie & Truth Revealed)

Seven: A Club Alias Novel

Knight: A Club Alias Novel

Doc: A Club Alias Novel

ALSO AVAILABLE IN THE CLUB ALIAS WORLD
Mission: Accomplished (Knight Novella Boxed Set)

Scary Hot: A Club Alias/Until Series Crossover

Moravian Rhapsody: A Club Alias Novella

A Lesson In Blackmail (A Black Mountain Academy Novel)

STANDALONES
No Trespassing

Dishing Up Love

COWRITTEN WITH CC MONROE
Steal You

Number Neighbor

A LESSON IN BLACKMAIL

Black Mountain Academy / a Club Alias Novel

KD ROBICHAUX

DEDICATION

*For Jenika and our mutual obsession
with Nate from Euphoria ;)*

CHAPTER 1

Nate

Skittish little mouse. That's what she is. With her thick-rimmed glasses perched on her cute, slightly upturned nose. Her light-brown hair falls around her face, and she doesn't bother pushing it back, instead using it as a curtain to shield herself. When someone approaches her circulation desk here in the school library, Ms. Richards quietly helps them with a small smile on her face, her full lips slightly twitching in the corners with nervousness, even though she's supposed to be the authority figure here. This is her domain, as Black Mountain Academy's librarian. Yet, she reacts to us students as if we're the boss of her.

Skittish little mouse.

I sit at a long wooden table surrounded by five other chairs filled with fellow upper crust students in my class. My six-three frame takes up more than my half of this side of the table, my arm laying across the back of Lindy's chair next to me. She's talking across me to Reese Trenton, who's pretty much the only true friend I've got in this place. Everyone else just wants a piece of me, being Nathaniel Jacobson Black

IV, great-grandson of the founding father of Black Mountain Academy. Hell, our family founded Black Mountain—period. Lindy's hand frequently brushes against my abs, even as she tries to flirt with Trenton, leaning over me to get closer to the both of us. Fucking ho. She's slept with three quarters of the swim team, me included.

I allow a second to think about if she knows we all call her an initiation to the team, not that she'd care. She wears her skank status like a badge of honor.

But my mind quickly turns back to who I'm actually infatuated with.

Ms. Richards.

Ms. Evelyn Richards.

Evie to her fellow staff members.

She's younger than the rest of the teachers. Twenty-two, maybe twenty-three. Yet she seems so much younger than even my eighteen years. She radiates purity, innocence, and it calls to the darkness inside me that wants to dirty her up.

My favorite part of the day is study hall, when I get to come to the library and fuck with her. I live for the hour in which I get to make her squirm. Nothing is better than leaning far over the circulation desk, forcing her to meet my eyes, only inches away from her delicate features, and asking the virtuous Ms. Richards in a low, gravelly voice where I can find a book on the Kama Sutra. And then hearing her stutter trying to get the words out that nothing like that can be found in the academy's library.

I'm sure half the things I say and do to her could be labeled as sexual harassment, but who's going to turn me in? The descendant of the very people she works for.

So I sit here and stare at her, like I always do, watching her try to ignore the heat of my gaze I know she feels, because every once in a while, she can't help but to look up and check to see if I'm still staring.

"Stop being a creeper," Trenton tells me when Lindy finally gives up and turns to face Megan in the other direction, and he punches me in the arm closest to him. "You're going to make that poor woman piss herself one of these days."

"It's just too easy," I murmur, catching her purse her lips as if she heard my voice but is still fighting not to glance this way.

"I've done some fucked up shit in my day, but this? This is low, man. Pick on someone your own size. She's like... half of you."

I can see him shake his head in my peripheral vision, never taking my eyes off Ms. Richards.

I smirk. "There's just something about her. She's nothing like the girls we've grown up with. The *hos* we're surrounded by," I tell him low enough only he can hear. "She's so innocent-looking. So quiet."

"Well... she is a librarian. It's kind of in her MO to be quiet. And innocent? I don't know about all that. Don't they say it's the quiet ones you need to watch out for? I bet she's a freak in the—"

Two things happen simultaneously at that moment. Ms. Richards turns a startled expression our way, having clearly heard Trenton's assessment, and the bell rings, cutting off what he was about to say and indicating study hall has come to an end.

But I don't move. My eyes narrow on her flustered features. What was she so startled by in his words? That two young men were talking about her in a sexual light, or was it that Trenton hit the nail on the head with his warning about the quiet ones?

She whips around to face away from us when she sees my measuring look, and I finally glance away from her to gather my books and stuff them in my backpack hanging on the back of my chair as I stand. I stick my pen behind one ear and lace my arms through the straps of my bag before shoving my seat under the table like a fucking gentleman, rolling my eyes when everyone else besides Trenton just leaves theirs out for anyone to trip on, for Ms. Richards to do their dirty work. He knows this shit makes me crazy and is a good enough friend not to fuck with me.

When everyone else makes their way to the door, I circle the table, pushing in all the other chairs, and I don't do it quietly, letting my frustration with everyone be known. A few look back at me as I grimace in their direction, having the decency to look a little guilty for acting like children who don't clean up after themselves.

I shove under the last chair, loudly skidding it across the tile floor and letting it smack into the wood of the table to drive my point home for them not to make the same mistake next time—not that they ever remember, spoiled, lazy-ass fucks. That's when I hear the sweet, timid voice come from the circulation desk, shocked that she's actually gathered the courage to initiate a dialogue between us, when usually it's me who begins our conversations with something that purposely makes her uncomfortable.

"Thank you, Nathaniel. You don't have to do all that. I'll get i—"

But I cut Ms. Richards off with a stern look, and her jaw snaps closed. I take slow steps toward her, allowing everyone to finally file out through the door of the library before I approach the desk. And then with the tone I know makes her squirm the most, I bend over, place my elbows on the surface, and grip my hands together as I lean toward her and tell her, "It shouldn't be your job to pick up after the senior class, *Ms. Richards.*" I feel a thrill go straight to my dick from the way she shivers at the sound of her name from my lips. "If we're old enough to be consenting adults—" I pause, letting the message behind my words take hold in her mind. "—then they're old enough to fucking clean up after themselves." I don't include myself in that last part, because I always take care of my shit, and she knows it.

She nervously pushes her hair out of her face and her glasses up the bridge of her nose, her eyes closed tightly behind the lenses while she swallows thickly. She nods in quick, shallow jerks of her head before she meets my eyes. "Th-thank you then, Mr. Black. N-Nathaniel. Better hurry before you're l-late for your next class," she responds, the same way she always tries to dismiss me after I've fucked with her.

"You're welcome, Ms. Richards." I trail my gaze from the top of her straight hair, down her white blouse primly buttoned to the hollow of her throat that just screams for my hand to be wrapped around it, over her small breasts and narrow waist, the gentle swell of her hips encased in navy slacks that hug her luscious thighs before the material flares at the knee, and end my perusal on her little leather flats with the rounded toes. When I meet her eyes again, she's practically panting with her anxiousness—and I can't help but fantasize her breaths coming out in this way if I were to drive my cock deep into her pussy.

"Have a good day," I finish before standing to my full height. When I hit my palm against the surface of the circulation desk, she jumps before nodding in response, not saying another word.

Skittish little mouse.

CHAPTER 2

Evie

I don't turn my head to watch him exit, but I can't stop my eyes from following his obscenely tall form as he makes his way to the door of my library before shoving his way through it. My library—I snort. It's not my library. It's *his family's* library. Nathaniel Black *the fourth*, heir to the Black throne upon their very own mountain the academy is nestled beside. Because if your family is rich enough to live there, high over the towns surrounding the mountain or in the neighborhoods nearby, then you're loaded enough to attend the private school his family built over a century ago. That boy... man is going to be the death of me. No really—he's going to give me a freaking panic attack that leads to my eventual demise.

He's done nearly everything to taunt me that I could possibly think of aside from actually putting his hands on me. Yet the words he uses along with his tone feel like a caress and a slap at the same time. Since the first day of the school year, my first day as the librarian of Black Mountain Academy, it's like he's made it his mission to... not quite bully me, but make me super damn uncomfortable. And what exactly could I do about it? After the first few weeks of it happening, I'd gone to report him to the principal, and he made it very clear that anything written up about a member of the Black family would be brushed under the rug so not to waste my time. I hadn't even gotten anything but Nathaniel's name out of my mouth before I was cut off and dismissed.

And as this is my dream job, I figured I could put up with him for a year, seeing as he's a senior and will no doubt graduate at the end of it. Because that is one good thing about Nathaniel Black IV—he's brilliant. Top of his class. Star athlete. Everything about him is perfect. Scarily so. *Obsessively* so. Aside from my degrees to become a librarian and a teacher, I took extra courses in psychology because I found the subject fascinating and even halfway considered becoming a school counselor at some point. It was easy for me to spot the clear signs of OCD in the young man. But having basically been muzzled when it came to this particular student, I kept my observations to myself.

His school uniform is always pristine. I once saw a food fight break out in the cafeteria, and he stormed out after something got on his shirt. He changed into a clean one he obviously kept stowed in his locker for such an occasion. He aligns his textbook, notebook, and three pencils *just so* at his place, at the same exact seat he sits in every study hour. He wears a pencil behind his ear between classes, as if to always be prepared in case he has to write something down in the hallway. Not to mention he always pushes in all the chairs every day as if he can't leave the library until it's back to the way he found it—the way I had it. I thought about testing a theory, leaving chairs out before his study hall group comes in to see what his reaction would be, but I found myself hesitating, as if afraid to catch his look of disappointment in me or something.

Which is utterly ridiculous. He's an eighteen-year-old high school student. I'm a twenty-two-year-old woman with *way* more life experience than he's had. Why should I care if anything I do disappoints him?

I will admit it was quite startling when Reese Trenton mentioned that it's the quiet ones like me who are the freaks. Quiet, yes, but it's taken years of therapy to come to terms with the fact that what I am is *not* freakish. If it weren't for Dr. Walker, I'd be lost, thinking these feelings and urges inside me made me the freak Trenton spoke about. Thank goodness the bell rang and snapped me out of it before I could correct what I heard. Because speaking about personal and sexual things with my students is obviously a no-no.

I spend the next hour returning books to their shelves and sending out email notices of books being late from students. Today is Friday, and there are no afterhours available to students, so I get to leave earlier—3:30—than every other day at 5:00 p.m. I'll open again early Monday morning as usual, an hour before school starts.

I love the fact that I get to go home early on Fridays. It gives me a chance to relax and prepare for the night at Club Alias, pretty much my weekly reward for getting through another five days as a functioning adult.

Oh, Club Alias. My happy place, my escape, my oasis. It's the one place I can go and shed the worries of my daily life and relax. As soon as I walk through that door, it's like the rest of the world just disappears. I'm no longer scared of my own shadow. All my anxiety fades away as soon as the darkly lit space swallows me up and I inhale the scent of leather and expensive colognes and perfumes. My hesitations disappear when I no longer have to make decisions for myself and allow the Doms to take away the responsibilities that weigh heavily on me. I let them make all the hard choices and just follow their instructions, trusting they'll make everything good for me. As long as I'm a good submissive, everything always turns out wonderful. I don't even have to think, just do. And since every single member of Club Alias has been vetted by a team of experts, including my therapist Dr. Walker, who is a co-owner, I trust every member wholeheartedly.

After the hour commute home, I lock my door behind me and hang my purse on the hook on the wall in the little foyer. I'm proud to say at twenty-two I own my own home. It's a small two-bedroom house in a nice little town I've called home my whole life. When my parents passed away a few years ago, they left me a small fortune in life insurance policies. The giant house I lived in growing up held way too many memories and was entirely too large for just me to live in and take care of, so I downsized to this adorable place I've slowly made my own. Each room has been a fun project to makeover, with only my yard and the kitchen left to go.

I walk past the first room I ever redid, the formal dining room I converted into my personal library, my dream room. Three of the walls are lined with floor-to-ceiling bookcases full of nearly every genre. There's a writing desk in the center of the room, and an overstuffed chair with a large ottoman in one corner where I spend hours getting lost between pages. A thick rug covers the wood floor that I love to squish between my toes. And there's a small side table next to the chair that's only large enough to hold a diffuser and my coffee. Yeah, it probably is weird to fill the room with relaxing lavender-scented steam and then hop myself up on caffeine, but that's just who I am as a person.

I pass through my living room and past my kitchen, making my way to my bedroom, where I toe off my ballerina flats and nudge them into the closet. I strip out of my blouse and slacks then shimmy out of my panties tossing them into the hamper beside my dresser. I unhook and let my bra fall down my arms, catching it in my hand before putting it in the top drawer where it goes with all the rest. I didn't sweat today, seeing as it's air conditioned in the school and a wonderfully mild temperature in the middle of autumn, so no need to wash my bras after every wear and wear them out. Those suckers are expensive. And while I have enough money to live comfortably for years to come if I don't splurge, thanks to my inheritance, undergarments are not something I want to waste money on.

Although there was one splurge I made, but I've definitely gotten my money's worth out of it—the five-figure membership fee for Club Alias. An extravagant amount to most people, but priceless when it comes to my mental health. I'd pay it over and over again for the peace it brings me, but luckily, it's a lifetime membership unless one breaks the rules and gets banned.

I, for one, am anything but a rulebreaker, so I won't ever have to worry about getting booted from my happy place. The rules of Club Alias are like *Fight Club*—you don't talk about it. You don't tell anyone about it unless you trust them to join, at which time you have to be their sponsor. You're responsible for them, and if they break the rules, it's on you. No one wants to get kicked out, so everyone is super cautious about the people they're willing to vouch for.

I personally learned about Club Alias through my therapist, Dr. Walker. After years of being his patient, he had me sign a non-disclosure agreement before telling me all about the club, where he thought I'd benefit more from than on any type of medication. And he was right. As long as I get my weekly dose, it gets me through the rest of the time without having to zombify myself with anti-anxiety and anti-depressants, which I'd taken various cocktails of since my parents died and never found the right combination for me. The club was the perfect prescription for me.

I pad into my bathroom and turn on the shower, letting the water heat up and making sure I have the right scented shampoo for my Dom of the evening. He prefers the fruity to the floral. After I've washed my hair, shave everything from my neck down, and soap up with my citrus body wash, I give everything one last extra rinse before stepping out and toweling off.

I wrap my hair up in a towel and slide my arms into my robe, tying the belt at the waist. I have a few hours to relax before I'm to be at the club tonight, and I plan on spending it in my comfy chair in my library, devouring the next VB Lowe book. Turns out, one of my favorite romance authors is a member of Club Alias and married one of the owners, so I get signed copies whenever she releases a new one. Which is quite frequently, if I think about it. I heard her talking one time about how her husband uses her word count as a game at home. I didn't stick around to hear the details, but there was something about sexy punishments if she didn't meet her goal for the day.

It sounded romantic to me, enough to make the tendrils of jealousy creep along the edges of my consciousness. And while I was having the greatest orgasms of my life every week, it made me uncomfortable to think about the loneliness I tried not to acknowledge when I was at home.

What would it be like to be in a relationship with someone who actually understands my needs? Someone who I could live this life with daily instead of having to wait for my weekly fix on Friday evenings. Sure, I could go any other day of the week if I wanted, but having to wake up so early during the work week—be there an hour before school starts plus my hour-long commute—doesn't really allow for me to go more often. And normally I'm so exhausted after my Friday night adventure that going back Saturday evening is just a no-go for not only my ladybits but also my psyche.

Being on the receiving end of a Dom's scene takes a lot out of a submissive, especially when those Doms are some of the best in the world thanks to Club Alias's initiation rules and training. Yes, aftercare goes a long way right after you're done to bring you back to reality from post-coital bliss, but I swear I need the whole rest of the weekend to feel halfway normal again by Monday. And that half-life high gets me through the rest of the week until Friday comes along once again.

But I'm not talking about having a relationship and doing full-on scenes every day. I'm talking about being with a man who understand my needs for submission in all aspects of my life. While I'm proud to be an independent woman, that doesn't make it any less exhausting. That doesn't make my anxiety any less, having to always be the only one there for myself, having to make every single little decision every moment of every day. For once, I'd like someone to be like *"Hey, I'd like a burger tonight. Want to come?"* Boom! Decision made about dinner and I didn't even have to waste any brainpower on it. Or like *"Hey, babe. The house is a wreck since we've been so busy. Let's start with the kitchen and work our way to the bedroom, where we can reward ourselves when we're done."* Sweet! Perfect! Plan made instead of having to wonder where the hell to start.

I bet Nate Black's room is never a wreck.

Um, whoa. I don't know where the hell that thought came from, but it needs to calm down with all that. I have no business wondering about anything having to do with that… guy. I don't even know what to call him. He's not really a bully. He's never done anything to actually hurt me or anyone that I know of. He's just… intimidating. Overwhelming. Definitely daunting and unnerving. Sometimes even menacing and straight-up terrifying—like when he slams the seats beneath the tables and gives his classmates that murderous look. But he's never turned that expression on me before. The only looks he gives me are full of mischief and seduction, long, unwavering stares that make me fidget in my own skin. I've tried to stop showing any outward sign that he affects me, but it's no use. I can't hide the fact that he gets under my skin with just a look.

I shake away my thoughts, knowing I have a whole weekend of not having to deal with Nate. I can put him out of my head until Monday when I go back to work.

I curl up in my library and pull the bookmark from between the pages, starting on the chapter I left off on and getting lost in the story, not fighting the arousal that consumes me during the explicitly detailed love scenes as I imagine myself in the heroine's place.

I choose to ignore the fact that my mind gives the Dominant hero the face of Nathaniel Black IV.

CHAPTER 3

Nate

I sit sprawled on Alistor's couch, the party getting started earlier tonight than usual, since no one really had any projects or homework to do this weekend. I sip my beer, not really tasting it, because my mind is stuck on one thing... well, one person.

Ms. Richards.

I've been approached no less than fifteen times since I got here an hour ago. Every time a chick looks up and sees me sitting here alone without one of my buddies, they come over and try to entice me up to one of the bedrooms, or to the makeshift dance floor, or out to the hot tub. But I've shooed each and every one of them away, uninterested, my mind on the one woman who won't leave my mind at peace when I'm not around her.

I don't understand my obsession with her. Not really. I get the whole wanting what you can't have aspect, seeing as she's an employee at the school I attend. And I get the whole older woman thing. But isn't the draw of being with an older woman to be with someone more experienced than you, to be with someone who can teach you a thing or two? The only thing Ms. Richards could teach me is the Dooey Decimal System, if I hadn't already learned that in elementary school. She's way too meek and innocent for it to be *that*.

But there's just something about her that calls to me, calls to my very depths, my need to control and dominate. The way she practically cowers gives me this heady sensation, makes my dick hard every time she shrinks away. Yet at the same time, the thoughts I have while I'm stroking myself in the shower to images of her melting beneath my touch, enjoying what I'm doing to her, not flinching from my hands... That's what always gets me off.

The thoughts of Ms. Evelyn Richards in bed with a guy like me is almost laughable in its awkward imagery. She wouldn't know what to do with everything I'd want to give her. She'd be terrified of my impulses. Of the things I crave. Of the way I'd use her body for my pleasure. If she's experienced anything at all, it's been nothing but sweet lovemaking with beta males with small dicks, I'm sure. She'd probably cry at the first thrust of my cock.

I dream of a day when I find a woman who can fulfill those parts of me, the parts I have to tamper when I've fucked the girls I've been with. I lost my virginity my freshman year to a chick on the dance team. After that first time of getting off with someone else, it awoke a realization inside me. While I lay there after I'd come, I didn't get the satisfaction everyone talks about. I still felt like something was missing, empty, as if the orgasm itself hadn't been the end goal after all. And I've spent the past four years searching for that missing link, all while holding back, not releasing my urges, which I know has *something* to do with what's missing.

If I were to act on my impulses, these girls would no doubt call me a monster. And while nothing would come of the accusations because of who I am, the tiny part of myself that's good and right doesn't want those rumors spreading around. Yeah, I'm known for being the bad boy, the tough guy, the fucker no one messes with. I've been called a fuckboy and a manwhore on my journey seeking to fill that emptiness inside me. But not one girl I've been with could ever accuse me of being anything but a great lover. They could follow it up with me being an asshole, casting them aside and not wanting anything more from them; they could say I was emotionally distant and didn't try to connect in any way other than physically. But not one of them could accuse me of hurting them, of doling out pain... like I really wanted to yet held back.

But in my fantasies, Ms. Richards takes it. She takes it, she likes it, and she begs for more.

"Fuck," I growl, looking down at my Apple Watch and seeing it's nearly eight. I wonder what Ms. Richards is doing right now. Probably at home, eating dinner on her couch, watching some documentary show on Netflix before going to bed by herself.

"It's the quiet ones you have to watch out for." Trenton's words replay in my head. And quiet is definitely one word that accurately describes Evelyn Richards. It makes her all the more intriguing when I think about her.

"Fuck it," I murmur to myself, standing and heading for the door, but not before tossing my empty beer bottle into the recycling bin in the kitchen. I sneer at some classmates as they knock over red plastic cups that are already starting to pile along every surface available.

As I gallop down the steps off the front porch, Alistor calls out to me, "Nate, where you going, man? That party is just getting started!"

I acknowledge him with a dismissive wave, pulling the keys to my truck out of my pocket, not bothering to answer him because the girl on his lap pulls his face into her cleavage as she throws her head back and laughs.

I slam my door behind me, sitting in the driver seat, and pull out my cell, staring at the time that lights up the screen. And then I make a decision.

A quick Google search gives me all I need to know. I don't even have to break out my sources at the school. I use the app to give me directions, cursing that my destination is almost an hour away, but I don't let it tamper this impulse.

I'm going to her house to see for myself just want Ms. Richards is up to on a Friday night.

I start the truck, set my radio for Bluetooth, and crank up the volume, choosing Submersed's *In Due Time* album to play. When the opening notes of "Hollow" fill the cab, I breathe out through my pursed lips, take in a deep breath through flared nostrils, and nod to myself once before putting the shifter in Drive and pulling away from the curb.

As Donald Carpenter's haunting voice sings about his soul being hollow and the person he loves being the only thing who can help him breathe, my foot grows heavier on the pedal, my speed picking up as I exit Black Mountain heading east toward the small town where Ms. Richards lives.

Every time a niggling thought tries to work itself into my consciousness about what a bad idea this might be, I shove it away, turning the music up louder, drowning everything out with the guitar solo in "Flicker."

Exiting when the automated voice indicates nearly an hour later, the album has restarted and "Hollow" is soothing the anxiousness inside me once again. When I'm told my destination is on my right only two hundred yards ahead, I turn down my music and hit the button to end the driving directions. And I see I arrived just in time to watch as Ms. Richards pulls her door shut behind her, locks it, and then hurries to her small but newer model car in her driveway. My windows are tinted to an illegal darkness, so I don't have to worry about ducking or anything as she backs out of her driveway then passes me on her way out of the neighborhood. Carefully, I do a three-point turn, keeping one eye on her car so I don't lose her before following her onto the main street, keeping a distance so she doesn't suspect she's being followed.

"Where are you off to, little mouse?" I murmur, merging onto the mostly empty highway and backing off a bit so she won't get spooked as I follow her when she exits.

Not ten minutes after we left her neighborhood, we're in the tiny downtown area of the town next to Ft. Vanter, an army base a few of the kids at my school talk about all the time, because their parents are high-ranking soldiers of some kind and can afford the tuition and daily commute to the academy.

I watch as Ms. Richards pulls into the underground parking garage beneath a three-story huge brick building on a corner lot, and I pull over on the one-way street, hoping no one runs me off before I see where she's going. I take a quick second to glance around at the business I'm in front of, seeing it's a pet groomer and their hours closed at six. A peek at the sign next me shows I can park here between the hours of 6:00 p.m. and 6:00 a.m. without getting a ticket, so I cut the engine and wait, my eyes never leaving the parking garage, hoping like hell there's not an entrance to the building beneath it.

But I don't have to hope for long. Soon, Ms. Richards in a knee-length black trench coat and heels she's most definitely never worn to school before comes up the flight of stairs on the side of the building that puts her at street level before she hurries to a door around front. She pauses next to it, pulling something out of her pocket... a mask? Yes, a black one she ties behind her head and adjusts it around her eyes, and then she disappears inside.

"What in the...?"

I hop out of my truck, beeping the locks, and make my way across the street to where I saw her enter. As I approach, I see there are two doors side by side. One has a sign indicating it's some kind of security business that closed at six, and the other is nondescript, not marked in any way. Even the windows have been blacked out. I reach out and tug, expecting it to be locked, but it's not. And I pull it open slowly, carefully, not knowing what the hell could be inside.

The interior is completely black and empty, but there's a staircase at the far wall, and as I step inside quietly, practically tiptoeing like a sleuth, the ceiling gives way to darkness interrupted by laser lights and strobes.

"What the fuck?" I whisper, approaching the stairs.

I take them one at a time, gently, slowly, not wanting to draw any kind of attention to myself.

"You're early tonight, Eve," I hear a female voice say over the low throb of music before my head breaks the surface of the second floor. I back up against the wall, staying hidden in the shadows, and listen.

"Oh, I guess I am. I was wondering why no one was at the door to check IDs. Guess I was a little excited to get here," she replies and giggles. She fucking giggles. It's such a sweet and carefree sound it makes me question if it was even her who made it.

The other woman asks her, "You meeting Master Connors tonight?

Y'all's scene last week was amazing. You took that bullwhip like a champ." And my head whips in the direction of their voices even though I can't see them.

Master Connors? *Scene*? *Bullwhip*? "What the fuck?" I repeat, wanting so badly to take a few more steps that would put my eyes above the second floor's ground level so I can see what the hell is happening.

"Thank you," Ms. Richards answers, and I can hear the shyness in her response, picture the blush rising in her face. "No, I'm meeting Lancelot."

"Ah, nice choice. I heard he's wonderful with a flogger. Have you gotten to scene with Scar yet?" the woman asks, and I don't have time to dwell on the mention of a flogger and yet another man's name before Ms. Richards responds.

"Twice. He did a great job, but I think my favorite so far has been Midas and his Hitachi. I could barely make it to my car my legs were so shaky." She giggles again, and my head is spinning. Because I know what a fucking Hitachi is. I've watched enough fucking porn to know exactly what the vibrating wand can do to a woman.

The woman laughs along with her. "Girl, same. How many did you get? I know he made you count. He makes everyone count."

"I got to six before I nearly passed out." She snorts. "I know, I know," she says, as if the other woman gave her a look. "I'm a wimp. Didn't Dulce get to like... fourteen or something?"

"Seventeen before she literally fainted. She's a badass."

And it's with that I realize the women are talking about orgasms.

Meaning Ms. Richards let a man bring her to orgasm six times with a vibrator before her legs were quivering enough she could hardly walk to her car to make it home.

I've heard stories about this town, rumors of their being a club here in which all one's sexual fantasies can be fulfilled. A BDSM club that only the super-rich and vetted can be a part of. But Ms. Richards... she's a fucking school librarian.

What. The. Fuck? Did I enter the Twilight Zone when I came through that door now behind me? Did someone slip something into my drink at the party, and now I'm hallucinating or dreaming on the couch, still in Alistor's living room? Because surely this isn't the real Ms. Richards. Surely this isn't the skittish little mouse who trembles in fear when I get too close.

I have to see for myself. I have to know for a fact what I'm hearing with my own ears will match what my eyes will see, because until then, I can't fully believe it.

"Let me take your coat and I'll check it. You need anything out of your pockets?" the woman asks, and I ascend three steps slowly, just enough to peek over the top step.

And my eyes land on the high heels I saw Ms. Richards was wearing while I was watching her from my truck. I try to take everything in at once—the dance floor, the DJ booth where all the lights are coming from, the bar, the horseshoe of giant leather booths, the red lights beyond them that look to be above different doorways hidden behind heavy black curtains, the glowing red neon lights at the very back of the club that has **Club Alias** in a classy curling script.

But my eyes shoot back to the high heel covered feet when I see them move slightly, and then my gaze trails upward just as Ms. Richards loosens the belt at her waist and unbuttons the row holding her trench coat closed. And then she lets the coat slip off her shoulders, catching it in her hands behind her, and she reveals what she's wearing beneath it.

"Fuuuck," I growl, my cock going rock-hard in an instant, so fast I wobble as all the blood from my head apparently drained straight into my dick. And then I curse again as both women's eyes turn toward my guttural voice, and I watch as the color drains from Ms. Richards's face.

CHAPTER 4

Evie

No. No, no, no. This can't be happening. My head jerks to the left, searching out where the deep curse came from, and I see just the head that belongs to none other than Nate Black as he peeks into the club, still on the stairway. I'm frozen like a deer in headlights as his eyes travel from mine down over my clothing—or lack thereof—to my feet incased in black pointed-toe stilettos.

His nostrils flare as his gaze moves back up, stopping at my breasts that are wrapped in dark-blue lace, unlined, so my nipples are clearly visible. It travels downward again, over my bare stomach, and stops for a moment at the matching dark-blue panties that are so tiny they're useless, only there for the barest modicum of modesty.

It's when his bottom lip pulls in between his teeth that I finally snap into action, hurriedly pulling my black trench coat back up my arms and over my shoulders and knotting the belt around my waist, not bothering to waste time on the buttons.

A word hasn't been spoken since his guttural curse, until finally Dixie, one of the submissives who works here, calls out, "Excuse me, sir. This is a private club. I'm sorry, but I'm going to have to ask you to leave." Her voice is polite but stern, yet Nathaniel ignores her, because why wouldn't he? Being who he is, he's been raised to do whatever the hell he wants.

Instead, he climbs the rest of the way up the steps, his frame coming into view one step up at a time, seeming to grow upward from the very depths of hell itself like a fallen angel, a demon. First, his chest. *Step.* Then, his waist, his torso encased in a fitted plain black T-shirt, a sharp contrast to the white polo shirt I see him in every day at school. *Step.* Next, his hips, which he reaches down at the front of to adjust what's behind his fly. *Step.* His powerful thighs wrapped in dark jeans, not baggy but not tight either, enough to be comfortable and able to move freely if he needed to get somewhere quickly. *Step.* Calves I've seen before when he was in his tiny swim uniform that look like they were chiseled by fucking Michelangelo himself. *Step.* And finally, black expensive-looking tennis shoes that seem so wrong in a place like Club Alias, where most of the men wear Italian leather dress shoes or boots.

He prowls up to me. No other word could be used to describe his gait. He's so tall and powerful-looking I can't move as he approaches, my head tilting... tilting... tilting back as he takes the final steps up to me so I can look into his eyes, one slightly hidden behind his dark hair that's fallen forward over his brow. I watch, fascinated, as the hair moves slightly when he blinks, caught in his thick, dark eyelashes, and then he runs his hand through it, pushing it out of his face and making his giant bicep flex as it comes up next to my head he's so very close. If I were to look straight ahead, I'd be staring at the middle of his chest. I swallow thickly, the sound of it loud inside my head even over the thump of bass playing low inside the club, since I got here early before it's even open like the lonely, desperate creature I am.

I don't know what to do, much less say. My student just saw me more than halfway naked inside a BDSM club—not that he knows what this place is. That is, unless he heard what Dixie and I were talking about before he made his presence known.

Oh God.

My humiliation grows tenfold.

A LESSON IN BLACKMAIL

I can't breathe. All I can do is stare up into the fiery gaze of the young man who spends every study hall hour making me want to scream in anxious frustration. My entire existence is trembling, vibrating. This is my happy place, my safe place, my haven. And now the sole person who I come here to escape from is here. Right here. Invading my sanctuary.

"Ms. Richards," he murmurs, his eyes darting between mine behind my mask.

I whimper, wanting to cry that he's caught me here. My mind not even wrapping around what this means. He could ruin everything. He could ruin my entire life if he told anyone.

"N-Nathaniel," I finally whisper.

Dixie speaks up again, clearly picking up that I am not in a good place mentally at the moment. "Sir, again, I'll ask you to leave once more before I call for security to escort you out." She lifts her cell, which I see out of my peripheral vision. I'm too scared to pull my eyes off Nate's, just like you don't look away from a snake or bear if you come upon one in a forest. You just fucking don't do it. As long as you keep your eyes on it, you'll be able to see before it attacks.

He lifts his hand up to my face, and I fight the urge to flinch. His hand is so big, his fingers so long and powerful, that it looks as if he could crush me without even trying. But as he turns his hand over to run a knuckle along my jaw, the first time he's ever laid a finger on me, his touch is gentle, feather-light, making the skin along my neck tighten with a chill.

I'm hypnotized, stunned stupid, unable to move a single inch as his eyes and touch hold me under his spell.

Move. Slap his hand away. Do something. He's one of your students! my mind screams at me, but my body refuses to listen, apparently awaiting what he wants, because as soon as the words leave his mouth, it's like someone disengaged the Pause button I was trapped by.

"Ms. Richards, would you mind accompanying me outside? Seems we have much to discuss," he says in a low tone, and my eyes dart to Dixie, who gives me a questioning look.

I lick my lips, taking in measured breaths now, trying to stay calm during what could be a disaster, a catastrophe, a complete crisis situation concerning my life, my entire existence.

"Y-yes, Mr. Black," I reply and watch as his brow lowers over his dark eyes.

"Very good, Evie," he rumbles, and the use of my nickname is startling, making me jerk at the same time his praise does something to my body I most definitely do not want to acknowledge. The heated tingle working its way down to my core has nothing to do with his commendation. Nothing.

As he spins on his heel and starts back to the stairs, my wide eyes turn to look at Dixie, who I'm sure can see the panic in them.

"Do I need to call one of the guys? Seven is right upstairs, and I'm sure Knight will be here any minute," she offers, but I shake my head before she even gets the whole question out of her mouth.

"No, it's fine. Everything is fine. Please, Dixie, just don't tell anyone, okay? I cannot lose my membership. I would.... I.... It would just not be a good thing if I didn't have Club Alias in my life, okay?" I beg, my eyes pleading, and she gives me a nod.

"You don't have to worry about that, Eve. I've got your back. If you need anything, all you have to do is ask, okay? You sure you want to go with that guy? He looked like he wanted to eat you alive," she whispers the last part, and my eyes dart between her and Nathaniel's retreating back.

I gulp, shifting on my feet. I have no idea what he's going to say to me, but I know I can't avoid what just happened. I can't simply go on about my night and weekend and then show up on Monday pretending he didn't just see me nearly naked in a nightclub, whether he knows what goes on here or not. But he's Nathaniel freaking Black. The smartest male I've ever met in my life by far. Scary smart. I'm sure he figured it out the moment he stepped foot inside.

"I'm sure. It'll be fine. I just need to talk to him about what he saw, and it'll be fine." I repeat "fine" a few more times, giving her a weak smile I know looks more like a wince before following Nate down the steps and out the door, onto the sidewalk.

He turns around, pinning me with his stare, and the force of his blazing expression sends me back a step, where I feel the bricks of the building close behind me. He paces a few steps before doing the same in the opposite direction, never taking his eyes off mine. Three steps down the sidewalk, turn on his heel, three steps up. I don't know how many times he does it, but I'm sure he does. I'm positive it's a certain number his OCD forces him to act out before he finally stops in front of me and glances down at my lips, the bottom one getting tugged to hell and back between my teeth. I'm pretty certain that flavor I'm tasting is my own blood I've drawn in my panic.

"Do you want to do this here?" he finally asks, and I break his stare long enough to glance in either direction. No one is out here at the moment, but people will start showing up any minute for our night of adventure.

"N-No. I don't think so," I reply quietly, needing to think five steps ahead, yet my brain hasn't even caught up to what is happening *right now*.

"Back to your house then?" he prompts, and I take a step back, straight into the brick wall that had been a foot behind me.

"*Back* to my house? You... you were there before? You f-followed me here?" My voice trembles. Not only had Nate invaded my happy place, but he'd also been to my home, my refuge?

Before I know what's happening, Nate reaches his big hand inside one of the pockets of my trench coat. When it comes up empty, he tries the other one, and I hold perfectly still, not wanting to force his hand to touch anything he shouldn't. He pulls out my keys from the second pocket, takes hold of my hand that is fisted at my side, unfurls my fingers, and places the fob in the center of my palm. "Get your car. I'll follow you back to your house," he orders, and everything inside me wants to jump into action to follow his instruction, yet I force myself to hold strong.

"I-I.... What is going on, Nathaniel? Why did you follow me? Why would you drive all this way—"

He cuts me off with a growl, leaning forward and trapping me against the front of the building, and palm slapping against the bricks on either side of my head and caging me in. It stills my breath he's so close, so overwhelming, taking up every millimeter of my vision. I see nothing but him, and I want to close my eyes and pretend I'm somewhere else, even though I know that's a lie I'm just telling myself, because I have no doubt I've never been this turned on in my life.

You should be ashamed of yourself. You freak. He's a student! Entirely too young for you.

I shake my head at my thoughts, trying to keep them at bay. I can't allow myself to shame what I'm feeling, to go back to thinking of myself as a freak.

"You're shaking like a leaf, Ms. Richards," he breathes against my ear before pulling back and looking me in the eyes. "Are you afraid of me?"

I look into the dark depths before me, seeing what I always see, the young man who likes to taunt me, practically torture me with his very presence every day. But there's something else in there, something almost... vulnerable, needy, as if begging for my help.

I decide to be honest. "Not of you, Nathaniel," I whisper. "Just... just of what you could do."

His eyes fall to my lips then meet mine once more. "And what's that?"

I swallow, trying to decide what I should say. What if he hasn't thought of all the things he could do with this information? If I tell him what I fear, it could just give him ideas. But of course, this is Nate Black we're talking about. I'm sure fifty different scenarios entered his brilliant mind the moment he saw what he walked into. So again, I go with honesty, because that's just who I am.

"You... you could ruin my life." I try to keep my voice strong, but the last word comes out in a whimper, my chin wobbling.

I hear people approaching from the side of the building where the underground parking lot is located, but Nate doesn't move. And the people don't say anything as they enter the club through the door right next to us, probably thinking we're a couple in the middle of a role-playing scene or something.

"You're right, Ms. Richards. I could." His gaze falls to my lips once more, and he leans in. I close my eyes, bracing myself for his kiss, my heart pounding in my chest so hard it makes my nipples hard beneath the lace of my bra. But the kiss never comes. Instead, I feel the sharp edge of his chiseled jawline against my cheek as he whispers in my ear,

"So how about we go back to your house and talk about what you can do to assure that doesn't happen." It's an order more than a question. And I nod in agreement this time instead of questioning him.

"O-Okay," I reply quietly, gripping my key fob.

He takes a step away from me, and I'm confused by my body's reaction. It's not relief I feel when he finally gives me space. It's a sense of loss I don't understand. As if my security blanket has been taken away from me, leaving me exposed and cold in the night. I shiver, even though the temperature outside is mild, so I tuck the neck of my trench coat closer to my chest.

"After you, Ms. Richards," he says, and gestures for me to walk before him in the direction of the parking garage entrance. We don't say another word to each other on the short walk up the sidewalk and around the corner, and I'm surprised when he follows me down the steps, because one has to have a special pass when you enter through the vehicle entrance for the gate to open. But then I realize he's not going to his own vehicle. He's escorting me to mine.

My doors automatically unlock when I get near it, and as my hand reaches out to grab the handle on my driver side door, Nate beats me to it, pulling it open for me. "Thank you," I murmur, folding myself inside. And then before I know what's happening, his big body is in front of me, taking away all of my oxygen he's so close, his form much too big for my little car. "W-what are you doing?" I squeak, and then I hear the click of my seatbelt being buckled.

"Don't worry, little mouse. Just making sure you're safe," he tells me, and his deep voice and the amusement in his tone make me shiver.

"Th-thank you," is all I can say as he slides himself back out, bracing one hand on the top of my door and the other on the roof as he stays bent to look me in the eyes.

He gives me a small smile that does little to ease my anxiety. It's more like the cat that got the canary, a dark and nerve-wracking but sultry edge to his expression as he watches me. "Be careful driving. I'll be behind you," he orders, and I nod.

"All right," I whisper.

"I overheard you say you were meeting someone here. It would only be polite to let them know your plans for the night changed."

My chin wobbles. Hot tears prickle the backs of my eyes. He's ruining everything. My one night that gets me through the rest of the week. My dose of submission that allows me to function and make decisions every other day. And the added knowledge that he did overhear Dixie and me talking just makes everything ten times worse. He now knows things about me I never wanted anyone else to learn, much less a student, far less my boss's son.

I don't realize a tear has escaped until I feel his gentle finger wiping it away from my cheekbone.

"Ah, don't look so sad, Ms. Richards. I'm sure we can work something out."

I don't know what to make of his words. Are they a threat... or a promise?

I guess I'll find out soon enough, because he steps back and closes my door, tapping the roof of my car like he does my desk every day after his parting words. And like always, it makes me nearly jump out of my skin. I blow out a breath and start the car, seeing him nod at me through the window before he turns and makes his way up the stairs to the sidewalk.

I send Lancelot a text apologizing, telling him I won't be able to make it tonight. He sends one back immediately saying he'll miss me but not to worry about it. I'm sure he has a line of submissives waiting for the chance to experience his flogging expertise.

The thought makes me bitter. If it weren't for Nathaniel Black IV, then I would be excitedly awaiting my Dom's arrival inside the club. Instead, I'm putting my car in reverse, backing out of the parking space, and heading home to see just how thoroughly Nate plans to ruin my life.

CHAPTER 5

Nate

Seeing her exit the parking garage, I pull away from the curb and fall in line behind her, no longer needing to keep a distance and make sure my presence stays hidden. She knows I'm following her, back to her house, back to where she spends her nights after she gets off work every day after I've spent an hour making her squirm.

Does she think of me once she gets home? Does she obsess over me the way I do her, never escaping my face even when I'm not around? Does she think of me when she lets those other men... do things to her, things that make her come over and over again?

My hands tighten on the steering wheel, my knuckles turning white, and my nostrils flare with rage and jealousy. It's ridiculous, I know, to be jealous over Evelyn being with other guys when I've been with just as many if not more girls. What's fucking me up is imagining this new reality, when I'd thought she was so innocent, pure, even virginal. How many times had I thought about taking her virginity while I'd fucked my fist? How many times had I pictured pulling out of her and seeing my cum mixed with her blood? Now I know that will never happen, and instead, Ms. Richards is....

No, I refuse to think of her as a freak. She's no more a freak than I am. She just obviously has needs that have to be fulfilled in a not-so-traditional way. A way that seems to be the opposite of mine, and the perfect match at the same time. She desires to be *mastered*? To submit and give herself over to someone and allow them to bring pleasure to her willing body repeatedly... until she can barely walk?

She's exactly what I never knew I could even dream of. Someone who would take my dominance happily, want it, crave it, get off on it over and over.

But I've never let that side of me loose before.

She's part of a club where... experts? Professionals? I mean, they spoke of a guy they called *Master*. And they said it with no type of humor or sarcasm in their voices. He was someone they respected, admired, *wanted to be under*. I've never even allowed myself to be rough with a girl, afraid I'd hurt her, not wanting to let the monster I keep trapped inside me escape and wreak havoc, even though every urge inside me had been to give myself over to it.

And the last person I'd ever want to hurt is Evelyn. I may love fucking with her with every fiber of my being. She makes me feel things I don't understand when she squirms and cowers. But I'd never physically bring her harm. I'd die before doing that. I'd kill before allowing anyone else to either.

But what if she likes the pain? The woman at the club said she enjoyed watching Evelyn's "scene" involving a bullwhip. I'm not sure what a scene is exactly, but a fucking *bullwhip*? There's no way a goddamn bullwhip could bring anything but excruciating pain to Ms. Richards's soft, smooth, perfect, and delicate flesh. Flesh I finally allowed myself to feel as I stroked her beautiful face, and then as I wiped away the lone tear she shed. Does she have scars hidden beneath those prim and proper clothes she wears at school?

No. No, I saw nearly every inch of her supple skin. The image of her standing there in that dark-blue lace underwear will be seared into my mind and spank bank until the day I die. She is a prudish, nerdy librarian by day, and a walking wet dream by night. And now my brain scrambles to come up with a plan. What will I say to her when we're back at her place?

"You could ruin my life," she whimpered. And it tugged at my heart I didn't even know I had. The fear and sadness in her voice, and the actual words she said. I'd murder anyone who'd even think to try to bring ruin to her life, but she doesn't need to know that. If she believes that about me, then that means she'll do what I want. She'll willingly do as I say if she continues to think I'll hold her secret over her head, ready to drop it at the first sign of her disobedience. But that'll never happen. I'll never do anything to hurt her—at least, nothing she doesn't beg for.

Minutes later, I pull in next to her car in her driveway. I lock my truck behind me and stride to her driver side door before she has a chance to open it, seeing through the window that she's gripping her steering wheel with both hands, her car still running, as if she's trying to decide if she wants to punch it in reverse and speed away from what's about to happen.

I can't let that happen. Not when I'm the closest I've ever been to figuring out things I've wanted to know about myself for years. So I grip her door handle and pull.

Locked.

My nostrils flare, and I bend to peer at her face through the window. When she turns her head to look at me, it's the terror I see in her eyes that keeps me from growling at her like I want to. Instead, I keep my voice low and even. "Come on, little mouse. Time to go inside."

It takes her a moment, as her eyes take in my whole face, and I soften my features, tamping back some of the anxiousness I feel to get her inside so we can finally talk. I give her a smile, one I hope comes across as friendly and soothing instead of the kind I usually give her that makes her squirm. It must work, because she finally nods, and when she turns off her car, the doors automatically unlock. I yank the handle quickly before she can have a chance to change her mind.

She unbuckles her seat belt then pushes a button, and her trunk pops open. I stand back, allowing her to get out and close the door herself before she walks to the back of her car. But I stay on her heels, ready to defend myself if I see she's reaching for some sort of weapon. Yet, she only pulls out her purse she'd locked inside while she was at the club.

I brace when she reaches inside it, my muscles tense and ready to strike if she pulls out pepper spray, or even a gun. But again, it's something harmless, just her keyring, seeing as her car's key fob had been separate when I handed it to her out of her pocket outside the club.

I pull the trunk closed for her, and she murmurs a quiet thanks before she starts up the walkway to her front door. Lights come on as we pass the sensor, illuminating the porch. My hands in my pockets, I stand behind her as she tries to ring the lock, but her hands are trembling so badly she drops her keys.

"Shit!" she hisses, and she glances behind her quickly, seeing how close I'm standing to her before facing the door once again. If she were to bend to get her keys, she'd have no choice but to press her ass against the front of my thighs, and she must realize this, because she seems to collapse forward, her forehead coming to rest on her front door as her shoulders sag—defeated.

I hear one soft sniffle, and it brings me to my knees, literally. I kneel behind her, reaching between her feet and grabbing the keys that landed on the welcome mat she's standing on, and I can't help but linger a moment, trailing a finger along the delicate bone of her ankle above the black leather of her sexy shoe.

She sucks in an audible breath, her back straightening above me, and then she turns around slowly, looking down at me. Her eyes are swimming with tears. She'd taken her mask off in the car, and it's the first time I've ever seen her without glasses on. She was intriguing and beautiful before, but as I look up into her face now from where I kneel at her feet, she looks like a broken angel. With our eyes locked, she stops crying, and I watch as hers bounce back and forth between my own. I feel at peace inside for the first time in my life, looking up at this woman as she stands above me.

When she holds out her hand for me to give her the keys, I unhurriedly stand instead so as not to spook her, taking the one that's shaped like a house and sticking it in the lock with a steady hand. I take a step back and gesture for her to continue, and she blushes and turns away to face the door once more with another quiet "thank you" before turning the key, twisting the knob, and pushing the door open.

She takes the key out and drops them into her purse and then hangs it on a hook on the wall of the small foyer. When she flips on the light, I shut and lock the door behind me and look ahead of her into the house.

It's small but clean, everything neat and tidy, and a part of me relaxes. She takes a few steps inside and flips on another light, illuminating a library, and I can't help but smile. Why wouldn't the school librarian have an impressive collection of her own?

"Um..." she starts, and I turn to face her. "I'm... I'm going to go change."

My hands in my pockets, I trail my eyes over her trench coat, remembering what's beneath it. I could make her take it off and stay in just her bra and panties. I know I could. She's that petrified of the information I now have on her. But that won't do anything to build trust between us. And I have a feeling that what I'm going to request of her is going to require trust too rather than fear alone.

"Where would you like me, Ms. Richards?" I ask, letting inuendo coat my tone, and I know she caught it when the blush rises in her cheeks once more.

She shifts on her feet. "Um... anywhere really. I have... well, I have the chair in there, or the couch in the l-living room." She takes a couple steps and gestures to something I can't see yet from this side of the wall. "Or... or the kitchen table is fine," she adds, pointing to the other side of her, where the kitchen is.

"Anywhere, you said? So you wouldn't mind if I joined you in your room while you change?" I taunt, lifting a brow, and smirk when her eyes widen.

"No!" she cries then clears her throat. "I-I mean, no, I'll just take a minute. Make yourself comfortable... out here." And then she spins around and hurries to the back of the house, disappearing into a room and closing the door behind her.

I chuckle to myself, strolling farther into her modest home until I'm standing in her living room. As small as the place is, I don't feel cramped. It feels cozy, everything in whites and grays with a dark-gray floor covered in a lighter rug. She has one comfortable-looking love seat and a matching chair, as if she doesn't really ever have company over, so she doesn't have a need for much seating. Peeking into the kitchen, I see the table is a two-seater, not four or six, and I realize she probably only has the second chair because it came as a matching set.

How lonely she must feel. Is that why she's part of a sex club, a place that would more than likely guarantee adult company? But with the masks she and the employee were wearing, and the ones the people wore who entered the club while I had her pressed to the wall, it seemed everyone wanted to keep their identities hidden. So it was just sex then? Because surely that wouldn't be a very viable way to meet people you'd want to start a relationship with, no one knowing who you are or anything about you other than your sexual appetite. One thing I've learned from hearing other adults talk is that a relationship based on sex has no potential of lasting. It's why my parents always tried to force into my mind that I shouldn't be having sex with girls I care nothing about. It would lead to nothing good, so I shouldn't be doing it.

Yet wasn't the plan I conjured on the ride over here basically the same thing? If she goes along with it, won't it just be a relationship based on sex?

No, there's already more to it than just sex, and we haven't even done anything yet. The feelings she provokes in me... they have nothing to do with sex, and I'll just have to find a way to sow those seeds along with everything else that happens.

In the end, I want Evelyn to be mine.

CHAPTER 6

Evie

What the hell am I doing? I should be... what? Calling the cops? Reporting him to the school? Telling his parents? No, no, and no. I can't do any of that. It would do no good. It would only end up with me being fired for trying to sully his name. As I was told the first time I tried to report him at the school, I shouldn't waste my time.

The best thing for me to do would be to just do as he asks, put up with him for the rest of the school year, and then he'll be off to college and will forget about me. Right? It's October. There's only a little more than two quarters left. I can handle that.

And as far as him being a student... he's eighteen. He's a consenting adult. If anything, I would be the one who could claim non-consent if it were to come down to it. Not that anyone one care. Not that anyone would believe me. But at least I couldn't be thrown in jail for inappropriate behavior with a minor. Because I have no doubt what Nate plans to do with me is highly inappropriate. The promise in his eyes, the threatening words against my ear, the innuendo behind the seemingly innocent things he asks. There's no way what he wants from me could be anything but sexual.

I pull out my drawer and tug on a pair of black leggings, and then I open my closet and grab a random tee, hurriedly taking off my coat and throwing on the shirt in case Nate has the bright idea to bust in my bedroom door. Not that it would matter. He's already seen me in nothing but my skimpiest under things.

I don't bother to take my contacts out. As much as I don't want to have this conversation with Nathaniel, I don't want to waste the time to change back into my glasses and leave him out there alone doing God knows what. I snatch a hair tie off the dresser and pull my loose curls into a high ponytail. So much for all the effort I spent hours on getting ready for the night.

Taking hold of my bedroom doorknob, I take a deep breath, say a silent prayer that this doesn't turn my life into a dumpster fire, and pull it open. I approach my living room cautiously, glancing around and not seeing Nate neither here nor the kitchen. I walk the short distance to my library, and that's when I spot him, over by my bookcases and paging through a book with a red cover. When I step inside, I focus on the story in his hands and see it's one of my favorite novels, *Brie Learns the Art of Submission* by Red Phoenix.

He glances up at me, closing the book and turning it over. It's a huge novel, a trade size paperback, but his large hands make it look tiny. When he focuses his attention on the back cover, not saying a word, my nerves finally get the best of me, and I collapse on my oversized ottoman and wait as he reads what the story is about. And when he's done, I take in the way he carefully replaces it exactly where I had it on its shelf.

He turns to face me, putting his hands in his pockets, looking relaxed, even though the air around me seems to be thick with tension. I wait, wondering what he'll say, imagining the worst as I try to think of what he could want from me, how he'll start off this conversation. So when he finally does, I jerk, sitting up straight at the sound of his deep, quiet voice. The first male voice I've ever heard inside my library, inside my home.

"Seems like a very educational book, Ms. Richards. Does there happen to be one on the art of dominance?" He asks this so casually, as if he's asking for a book on bird watching, or if I can direct him to a cookbook he might enjoy, hell, anything other than the lifestyle I lead.

I fidget with the hem of my T-shirt in my lap, not knowing exactly how to respond.

"Um... I've... I've never really looked into it before. That's not something I'd personally need to read up on, so you wouldn't find it in my collection," I tell him nervously.

I watch as he strolls over to my writing desk, takes hold of the back of the rolling chair, and pulls it from beneath the desk. I think he might take a seat there, but he doesn't. Instead, he pulls it around until it's in front of him, and then he pushes it to a stop right in front of me. He lowers himself into it, his big frame making it squeak as he settles his weight into it. His legs are spread on either side of mine, so when he uses his feet to wheel the chair closer to me, my legs are trapped between his and the ottoman I'm sitting on.

He's so close, closer than he ever was at school, when I always have the circulation desk to hide behind. But not as close as he was half an hour ago, when he had me pressed against the building of the club.

I can't take the tension anymore. I have to get this conversation going or I'm going to have a panic attack, and then there won't be any talking whatsoever. "Nathaniel..., what is it you want from me? Please. Just... tell me what you're going to do."

When I meet his eyes, it's not the look of a feline in this cat-and-mouse game we've always played like I expect. There's a seriousness in his features, a barely whispered plea for help that's there for one split second before he hides it behind a slow smile that raises goose bumps along my arms and neck.

"You know, I've always thought you're pretty, Ms. Richards." He lifts his hand and traces the line of my jaw, and I shiver. "And then I thought you were sexy as fuck when I saw you basically naked at the club and with your mask on." His fingertip trails down the column of my throat before it hooks into the neckline of my tee. He pulls it out and lets go, and it snaps back into place. "But you, here, in comfortable clothes, your hair pulled back from your face for once instead of hiding behind it and without your glasses?" He reaches behind me and tugs gently on my ponytail. "You're the most beautiful creature I've ever seen," he rumbles huskily. And the way he says it, with the look on his face, for some reason, it comes across as sincere. It doesn't sound like the taunting tone he uses when he teases me at school. His compliment is genuine, and I blink in surprise.

"Th-thank you." I blush. I don't know what else to say. No one's ever told me something like that, unwavering, right to my face before.

His smile is soft this time, a real one that reaches his eyes. "You're welcome." He glances down to my lap, where I'm wringing my hands, and he takes hold of them in his, the sheer size of them engulfing mine and making them look like a child's. "Ms. Richards... Evelyn. Can I call you Evelyn when we're outside of school?" he interrupts himself to ask politely, and it's so against his normal character of doing as he pleases that I squeak out a reply before thinking about the consequences.

"Yeah, that's fine."

He chuckles, the sound making my veins vibrate beneath my skin. "Awesome." The use of the word reminds me that even though he's a huge, intimidating, sometimes threatening man, he's also just an eighteen-year-old with a past I really know nothing about. "Evelyn, what I want from you, in exchange for keeping your little secret—" I swallow as he lowers his head but looks up at me from beneath his thick eyebrows. "—is for you to teach me everything you know about Dominance."

I shake my head shallowly, my brow furrowing in worry. "I... I told you, I don't know anything about that. I'm... I'm a submissive," I admit out loud, and my heart gives a little flutter at saying the words openly to someone outside the club. "I'm on the total opposite end of the spectrum. I don't... understand a Dominant's need for control. I can't teach you anything about that. I'm... I'm programmed with the contrary. I hate control. I despise it. It's the bane of my existence, having to make decisions day in and day out." I'm trembling, and suddenly I'm word vomiting everything I've only ever told one other person in the whole world, my therapist.

And Nate just holds my hands tighter, narrowing his eyes and taking it all in. No longer threatening. He's absorbing every word out of my mouth, his grip on me keeping me grounded, so I keep going.

"A Dominant..." I shake my head, trying to find the right words. "A Dominant is like the yin to my yang, my other half, the perfect opposite. Everything that I hate, that makes me anxious, that makes me panic, has the opposite effect on them. Control of situations, being a leader, having people rely on you, mastering a scene—"

"A scene. What does that mean exactly? I heard you and the other girl talking about a scene at the club," he asks, and he has his studious face on, the one I've seen him wear in classrooms I've come by when dropping off books and media needed for a teacher's lesson. It's like he's zeroed in on what's being taught, taking it in, pulling it apart and learning all its parts at a quantum level inside his mind. This is why he's so brilliant, why he's the top of his class and not just popular and athletic.

For some reason, it makes me relax a little. This question... I can answer this. I *live* for this. I know this like I know where every single book in my personal library is placed.

"That's what we call it when we're at the club and we act out a preplanned... well, *scene*, or scenario. From the moment we begin the... sexual activity—" I flush hotly, looking away from his eyes and down at our hands still joined against the tops of my thighs. "—until we reach completion, that's the scene. And then a..." My eyes widen and I look up, realization hitting me. I do know something about Dominants I can tell him. "And then a *good* Dominant treats his submissive to what is called aftercare."

His head tilts to the side, and I have to admit the look is adorable. "Aftercare," he echoes. "I assume that's the care he'd give you after the scene is complete. As in, what? Cleaning up? Redressing you?"

I give him a shy half smile. "Yes and no. The first part, yes. But it's more... Hm. Let's see. It's hard to explain in words. This is the first time I've ever tried to describe it to anyone."

"Take your time, Evelyn. I want to learn," he urges, and the way he's looking at me does something electrical to my blood.

I nod. "Okay, well. I need to go back a little further then. During a scene, if the Dominant is skilled in what he does, then it's not just like any old sex. It's not just... wham, bam, thank you, ma'am, you both get an orgasm if you're lucky, and you're done with it." I shake my head and then close my eyes, hating how awkward I am.

He pulls me out of my self-deprecating thoughts with a squeeze to my hands, making me meet his gaze once more. "Good, all right. It's not normal fucking. Then what's it like?"

The use of the F-word from one of my students is startling and I flinch. I swallow, trying to get back on track. "Right. So... it's way more than that. More sensual. More... everything. It's not just physical. You're meeting each other's needs. I'm meeting the Dom's needs by submitting to him, letting him take control, allowing him to do things to me willingly. He's meeting mine by not forcing me to have to make decisions. I'm giving in to what I trust is his expertise. I don't have to think about it. I don't have to learn anything about him. I can just know he's going to take care of me and bring me pleasure. At least... at Club Alias that's how it is." I shake my head, getting back to answering his question.

"Anyway, so when you get out of your head and give in to all those things, it allows the pleasure to escalate beyond the normal measures. It elevates you, like... for a submissive, it's almost a trance. Like... an out-of-body experience. You feel like you're floating in another dimension." My cheeks explode with heat at how enthusiastic my voice has gotten, and I realize to a normal person I probably sound ridiculous, talking about sex taking you to another dimension.

But I'm not speaking to just some normal person, now am I? No. And I know that, because he pulls our joined hands closer to him, setting them on his thighs now, and it tugs me toward him.

"That sounds amazing, Evelyn. Truly. So what happens then?" he encourages, devouring my every word.

"Well, that out-of-body feeling is what we call subspace. And it's important to come down from that... like, gently. It could be rather jarring to go from floating in another world to suddenly crashing into reality, right? So a good Dominant will provide aftercare, to slowly bring his sub back into her body, to make her feel warm and welcomed back to earth basically." I smile, thinking about some of the amazing Doms I've been with. "Personally, aftercare is my favorite part of the whole experience. It's what leaves me feeling centered and levelheaded and gets me through... the rest of the week." I finish up the sentence differently than what I'd been thinking, not wanting to mention he's partly the reason I need such extreme measures to help me function like a normal adult.

"You make it sound like getting a fix, like a dose or treatment," he replies, his expression curious.

I nod. "For me, it is. Not... not to get into my history or anything, but medications for my mental health didn't work out so well. And this is the only thing that's ever made me feel halfway... normal."

"Normal." He chuckles. "They say it's the quiet ones who are the freaks." He grins jokingly, but the word sinks to the bottom of my gut like a lead weight. I try to jerk my hands out of his grip. But he holds them hostage. "Ms.— Evelyn, what's wrong?" Nate asks, holding tighter as I try to pry my hands away, leaning back on the ottoman with all my strength, but he pulls me forward easily as if I weigh nothing. "What did I say?"

"I'm..." I shake my head, my heart shockingly hurt for some reason, after I'd opened up to him. "I'm not a freak," I manage to whisper, and I feel the corners of my mouth wobble as I try to fight back the sudden urge to cry. "Being submissive does not make me a freak. Just like being a Dominant wouldn't. Just like having to control things, keep things neat and tidy and perfect, and count to certain numbers in your head, doesn't make *you* one!" I cry out. And if I had my hands free, I would've slapped my palm over my mouth, in shock at the shit that just came out of it, but I don't. So I can only look at him in wide-eyed, slack-jawed horror.

I brace myself when I see his nostrils flare, his brows lowering over his eyes that have gone dangerously dark. I've blown it. I just know it. All he wanted was to learn about Dominance and submission, and I had to go and spaz out and throw his own quirks in his face like an asshole. Hurt me and I'll hurt you back, like some child playing slaps.

But this isn't some game. This isn't some harmless conversation we're having for funzies. This man holds my entire life in the palm of his hand, and he could crush everything I've worked for with one sentence from his mouth to his family, to my boss.

I hold my breath, waiting for his retaliation, every muscle in my body tense...

CHAPTER 7

Evie

The next thing I know, in one fluid movement, he rolls the chair he's sitting in away, just enough that he can bring his long legs that were on the outside of mine together, forces them between my knees, and then uses his grip on my hands to yank me forward and onto his lap, straddling him. He takes my hands and circles them behind my back, locking them in place with his at my tailbone. He's so tall that even as I sit on top of his lap, I still have to tilt my head upward to look into his eyes, which I do, but not for long, as his mouth comes crashing down on mine.

I'm so shocked by this turn of events, by this unexpected switch in emotion, that I freeze, trying to let my mind catch up with what is happening in reality instead of what I feared would take place by throwing those words in Nathaniel's face. But then his mouth opens over mine, and his hungry growl sends of hot wave of wetness straight to my pussy. I don't think; I just feel, and I open my mouth to receive his tongue, giving in to who I am inside and submitting to his dominance. This, I can do. This, I'm really fucking good at—giving over control and letting him take what he needs from me.

And what he needs from me right now is my tongue as he strokes his against mine in a way I've never been kissed before. There's not a lot of kissing that goes on at the club, as far as the scenes *I've* ever participated in. Kissing is usually reserved for the people who are in actual relationships, a form of intimacy not often shared between random people who are scening together. At least in my experience. So Nate's mouth on mine is an unfamiliar pleasure, and I melt into him, letting him lead me through a dance of lips and tongues, sighs and stolen breaths.

With another ferocious growl from deep within his chest, he launches me backward onto the oversized ottoman, following me with his big body as he pulls our still joined hands above my head. His weight is heavy but comfortable between my legs, and I whimper as he grinds his hips, the erection behind his fly notching perfectly with my clit covered by nothing but thin layers of lace and cotton. His face hovers over mine as he watches me, like he always watches me, and his dark hair hangs forward, creating a shadow over one side of his face. He's like a gorgeous incubus come to wreak havoc.

He grinds his hips again, and it steals my breath, my head pressing back into the cushion as I arch my body closer to him. I need release, been waiting all week for my release, and he stole it from me, and I'm so desperate for it now that I don't even care it's him who could give it to me right here, right now.

"Please," I beg before I even realize the word falls from my lips, and I tighten my fingers between his above my head, drawing my knees up and placing my heels on the edge of the ottoman so I can press my pussy against him harder.

I feel his muscles tighten above me, and I watch as something inside him loosens, rolling up and folding away like an accordion, as he lets go of the tight control he must have had a rein on. Because something inside Nate Black snaps, and he lets out a sound almost feral as he slams his mouth to mine once more.

He thrusts hard against me, making me shudder and my eyes roll back in my head as he devours my mouth. "Fuck," he growls against my lips, and if we were naked, I'd be sore with how powerfully his hips thrust against mine. But I love it, and I take it happily. When I look up into his eyes once more, I see... I see so very clearly he wants something, but he doesn't know how to ask, how to make it happen. This is why he was asking me to teach him. This is what he doesn't know how to let loose but still maintain control over. He has urges, needs that he doesn't know how to fulfill, and he was hoping for my help.

My submissive stretches and purrs as she unfurls beneath him, swishing her tail and ready to teach him exactly what he needs to know to satisfy both of us.

"That's it... Mr. Black," I tell him, remembering the sensual look that covered his face when I called him that before. "Don't think. Just feel. Do whatever feels right. Trust yourself, and give in to what your body craves. Tell me what you want, what you want me to do. You're not gonna hurt me. *I can take it*." I whisper the last part, and as I watch my words sink into this brilliant man's mind, seeing them give him peace he's been searching for, for who knows how long, I relax into the soft cushion beneath me and give myself over to him, and it's like coming home.

"Fuck, Evie. Keep your hands there and don't move them," he murmurs, almost tentatively, as if he doesn't believe I'll follow his orders without a fight.

"Yes, Sir," I reply, even though I know I don't have to. But if this is what he needs, if this is what I can do to build his confidence and help him grow into a good and respectable Dominant, then that's what I'll do. I'm an educator, after all. And I try not to think about the fact that this isn't the only way Nathaniel Black IV is my student.

He puffs out a single huff of amusement as he lets go of my hands, and when I keep them right where he left them like I'm supposed to, I see him relax slightly.

It's not until he lifts himself off me, stands between my legs, and reaches behind him to grasp the neck of his shirt and tug it over his head that it hits me exactly what I'm doing.

Am I going to have sex with Nate?

I've been so caught up, so overwhelmed in the last several minutes that it's just now dawning on me—I'm not at Club Alias with one of the vetted members who have been cleared as safe to be dominated by. There is no security around, no other members to help me in case of an emergency. This is my home. This person is a student at the school where I work. He's inexperienced in the D/s lifestyle and could easily hurt me, since he's never been trained in dominance.

But for the life of me, I cannot seem to care enough to stop this. Maybe it's because I'd had my heart set on the release I was guaranteed to have tonight, like every Friday night. Maybe I'm so desperate for my dose of submission that I'm willing to get it from anyone. But something inside me whispers that the real reason is because I want Nate Black. I want him like I've never wanted anyone before in my life. And I want to teach him everything I can about being a good and proper Dominant, so he can be mine.

When his shirt is off, he swipes his fingers through his hair before folding the black fabric neatly and placing it into the rolling chair behind him. I suck in a breath at how freaking perfect he is. He's tall and lean but wide, the most beautiful swimmer's body I've ever seen. His chest is bare of hair or ink, just flawless, smooth, light-tan skin.

I lose sight of him as he drops to his knees, and he takes hold of my leggings. I feel the elastic of my panties pop back against my skin as he decides to leave them on before tugging my black bottoms down my legs. He lets go of the waistband and pulls them off the rest of the way by the elastic at my ankles, so they stay right side out, and he easily folds them and places them in the chair with his shirt. He looks down on me, hands still right where he told me to keep them, my dark-blue lace panties only enough fabric to cover my very center.

He suddenly looks lost, like he's stuck and doesn't know what to do. Like he's fighting himself, battling what he thinks is right versus what he craves. I take pity on him and tell him gently, "Normally, a Dom and a sub would have preplanned their scene. They go over each other's likes and dislikes, what's expected from each participant. In a normal scene, you wouldn't be second guessing everything, Mr. Black."

His eyes meet mine and he stands tall, squaring his shoulders over his hips. The stance looks powerful, especially from my prone position beneath him. "Tell me more," he demands and crosses his arms over his chiseled pecs.

I swallow at the beauty of him. "Um... well. The Dom and sub would have discussed what they'd like to happen during their time together. Whether there would be toys involved and which ones. Whether there would be actual intercourse, or oral, or... anything really. You'd know each other's hard limits, which are things that are completely off the table. You'd know the things the sub is open to experimenting with. Oh! And you'd have a safe word."

He gives me a sexy smirk that makes my toes curl into the cushion. "What's your safe word, Ms. Richards?" he asks, and it's the same tone he uses when he fucks with me at school.

I meet his stare head-on and unwavering. "Periodicals."

He snorts. "Of course it is, my little library mouse."

It's not the first time he's called me his mouse. And I have to admit, I don't hate that he's given me his own little nickname, which after the way he told me he thinks I'm beautiful, I choose to take it as a term of endearment rather than a putdown.

"What are your hard limits?" he asks, widening his stance and giving me that studious face of his.

I swallow. "Right now, and in this precarious position, there are too many to list. Things you probably wouldn't even think of or need to."

"Like what?" he demands.

"For one, urine and fecal play," I say haughtily and snort out a laugh at his grimace. But then his face morphs into a mask of seriousness, and before I know what he's doing, he bends over me, skims his hand under my shirt and beneath one cup of my bra, and he pinches my nipple. I whimper at the sharp pain, my head throwing back into the ottoman even as my hips rotate against the sudden weight between my legs.

With my eyes closed, I can only hear that he hovers above me, but his silky voice sends goose bumps up my spine when he tells me, "Might want to watch your tone, little mouse. I don't do well with being sassed and laughed at."

I don't hesitate. "Yes, Mr. Black." And he groans in pleasure, whether at my whispered words of submission or at his cock nestling up against my hot pussy, I don't know. Maybe both.

But then I hear his intake of breath, and I open my eyes to see doubt in his. "I'm... I'm sorry, Evelyn. Did I hurt—"

"No," I cut him off. "Do not apologize. You did exactly what you were supposed to. I deserved that small punishment for doing something against your wishes. You didn't overreact. You did nothing wrong. And... *I liked it*." I shudder as he circles his fingertip around my now sensitive nipple.

He nods, his confidence back in place. "Now, is there a way we can fast-forward through the preplanning stuff for right now, because now that I have you half naked and under me, I really don't want to take a timeout to learn everything in one go," he murmurs against my neck, just below my ear, and I shiver.

I give a frantic nod, unable to keep my hips still as I work my clit against the rough line of his fly. "You... you know that kids game Red Light, Green Light?"

"Yes," he says and then licks a path from my earlobe to the hollow of my throat.

"If you're worried you're doing something I don't like, you can ask me 'Color?' and I'll say green, yellow, or red. Green is go, yellow is take it slow, and red is stop immediately. You do not punish a submissive for calling their safe word or red. It's a matter of trust, of being a good Dominant. It is your job to keep your submissive's trust no matter what *you* may want. Her safety, physical and mental, come above all."

He places a kiss at my jaw. "It sounds like the sub is the one who might actually be in charge."

"The Dom is in control of the sub. The sub controls how far she'll allow the Dom to take her. The better Dom you are, and the better you are to your sub, the more she'll give you, the more she'll let you take from her. Yin and yang," I explain and end on a mewl as he thrusts against my panty-covered core. Just a few more moments of grinding against each other and I could come oh so easily.

"Color, little mouse?" he asks, rocking his hips between my legs once more.

"Green," I whimper, fighting the urge to lower my arms around him and hold him to me.

As if he read my mind, he grasps one of my hands, but he doesn't place it around him. He tilts his body to one side and trails my palm along his smooth flesh, down his chest, the ripple of his abs, over that thick V of muscle, and then over his jeans to grip his cock.

"*Fuck*," we both say on an exhale at the same time, but neither one of us laughs.

I've been with men of all shapes and sizes in my time as a submissive, but I don't think any of them have ever come close to the sheer massiveness I currently hold in my hand. There's no way my hand could even circle his girth, even if he were bare. It makes me want him desperately, to test and see if I can take all of him. I want to feel the burn and stretch as he forces himself into me, and the thought alone makes me shudder beneath him.

"Enough of this, Evie. Here or in your bedroom?" he asks.

And I look him in the eyes with a little shake of my head. "You're in control, Mr. Black. Whatever, wherever you want."

CHAPTER 8

Nate

"You're in control, Mr. Black. Whatever, wherever you want."

Her words would bring me to my knees if I weren't lying on top of her. She's giving me everything I've ever craved.

"You're not going to hurt me. I can take it."

I'd nearly come in my pants the moment that part had left her lips. But I wasn't going to ruin this like some virgin seeing a tit in person for the first time. This was my first time being allowed to do everything I desire. As comfortable as it is in here, something inside me wants to take her in her bed, to be surrounded by her things, mark it with my presence and what I'm going to do to her so she'll never be able to sleep in there without thinking of me.

I slide my arms beneath her and use the power of my legs to stand us both upright, and her legs automatically lock behind my back. She's still following my orders, one hand pressed to the front of my jeans and the other fist resting atop her ponytail. Fuck, she's good at this, such a good little submissive. How did I get so fucking lucky?

"Put your arms around my neck," I tell her, and she does without hesitation. It brings the front of her up against my chest and abs, and the softness of her tits behind her T-shirt makes me feel powerful. She's so tiny, delicate, with gentle curves, everything so feminine, and it makes me feel all the more male with her wrapped around me.

I carry her back to the room I saw her disappear into earlier and close the door behind us, even though we're here alone. It makes it feel more forbidden, being enclosed in the room alone with Ms. Richards. Evelyn. Before tonight, I'd never been alone with her but for the briefest of moments when everyone exits the library. And now I'm here in her house, in her bedroom, and I'm about to get her naked.

I guide her down my body until her feet touch the floor, unraveling her hands from behind my neck, and take a step back from her. She waits for my instruction, and I'm overwhelmed with the possibilities. Not wanting to seem like some inexperienced chump, I'll go with the things I've fantasized about over and over. If I have it my way, we'll be checking off many things on my list of the positions and scenarios I've imagined her in. But for now, I'll start with the one that never fails to get me off.

I take a few steps backward until I meet the wall and lean against it, crossing my ankles and then my arms over my bare chest. The lights are dim, only a small lamp on near her bed, so I'm in the shadows while she's more lit.

"I've fantasized about this moment since the first day of school," I admit in a low tone. "That first time I walked into your library for study hall, and you introduced yourself as the new librarian. And then you gave that little speech about it being your first job, right out of college. How it was your dream job." She narrows her eyes as she tries to see me clearer, but I know my features are hidden in the shadows. "I knew it was my family who had given you your dream job, and for some reason, it made me feel like you were indebted to me. In a roundabout way, I had made your dream come true."

She doesn't say anything, and I can see her fighting the urge to fidget, to stay in her role as my submissive. I continue on, wanting her to know more about me.

"You show up to school every day in your perfectly pressed blouse and pants, your pretty little shoes, your hair straight and neat, your nails never even chipped. For a guy like me, who needs order, who needs things straight, and clean, and aligned, and perfect... you were easy to become obsessed with. And then the first time you cowered from me, flinched away at a loud noise I made, blushed at the shit I say to you... it made me feel powerful. Powerful in a way I've always craved but never had an outlet for. Unable to give in to these... desires, these urges," I tell her, still keeping my voice lowered, even, not wanting to scare her, while I confess how fucked up I am.

"I've fucked countless girls, Evelyn."

She flinches then, and I don't know if it's because I dropped an F-bomb or if it's because she doesn't like thinking about me with anyone else.

"I've lost track of how many girls I've been with. But I have always, always kept a tight leash on what I've always thought of as a monster, a beast inside me. Afraid to get too rough. Worried I'd accidentally hurt them. It's always been soft touches and steady, measured movements. Gentleness. And while they've all seemed to enjoy that, seeing as they always want to come back for more, it leaves me unfulfilled, unsatisfied. Empty. Yeah, my cock got off—" I step out of the shadows and closer to her, and I see her leg muscle tense and relax as she denies her instinct to take a step back. I approach her slowly, languidly, liking the way she holds my gaze, even though I see the fear mixing with her desire for me. "—but it did nothing for my soul. I didn't feel anything in my heart. It felt like something was missing, like I was doing it all wrong. And then I met you."

I trail my fingertip along her jaw, tipping her chin up when I reach it. "And my fantasies of the things I wanted to do to you filled my head while I stroked my cock made me come so good, so thoroughly. To the point that I got more fulfillment, more satisfaction from fucking my own fist than I ever did fucking any of those other girls." I lean down and press a kiss to her lips. Gentle this time, instead of the ones I surrendered to in her library. "And so I haven't been with anyone else since that first time I fucked you inside my mind, because I knew it was pointless. No one could measure up to you, Evelyn." I whisper the last part, looking deep in her eyes, and it has the exact effect I was hoping for when I told myself I should be honest with her.

She melts against me, and I hold her against my front, taking her mouth in a long, lingering kiss that makes her like putty in my hands. When I pull back and let her go, her eyes look almost drugged, glossy with arousal.

"Take off your shirt," I order, and she doesn't hesitate. She crosses her arms and grasps the hem of her shirt, pulling it over her head and tossing it next to me. My nostrils flare with immediate rage until I turn my head to see it landed perfectly inside the laundry hamper. When I look back at her, she's fighting a smile. My eyebrow quirks, and she instantly schools her features. "Bra next."

She reaches behind her, even as her cheeks turn a pretty shade of pink in the dim light, and she curls her shoulders forward, allowing the straps and cups to fall into her hand. My heart thuds in my chest. She's so good at this. Knowing how I am, how I crave tidiness, she doesn't drop it to the floor, but she doesn't move. I can tell she's considering what to do with it, but since I haven't given her another order, she doesn't want to break her role and just keeps it in her grasp. Since she's not tossing it into the hamper, it must go somewhere else. And if it's anything like the rest of her house, there's a place for everything, and she likes everything in it's place. Maybe not as obsessively as I do, with measured precision, but still, good enough that even I could live with it.

I hold out my hand, and she places the delicate lace in my palm. "Where does it go?"

She licks her lips, and my cock twitches. "Top right drawer."

I turn around and pull it open, seeing a vast number of bras in a multitude of colors, fabric, and shapes, all lined up neatly in rows. I see the exact spot she'd pulled the one she wore tonight from, and I carefully replace it, then close the drawer. With my mind not obsessing over the garment, I finally take in her bare breasts. Each one is the perfect mouthful, and I can't wait to suck those little pink nipples between my teeth, to watch her react like she had in her library when I pinched one for having a smart mouth.

I could have her undress me, but I don't want to waste time with her wondering what I'd want her to do with my clothes, so I'll do it this time, so she'll know how I like it. I make my way over to her bed to sit on the end, untying each of my shoes before toeing them off. I take off my socks, folding each in half and tucking one inside each shoe. I stand and walk back over to her dresser, setting the pair neatly on the floor in front of it. I unload my pockets, aligning my wallet, keys, and phone in a straight line on top of the dresser next to her jewelry box, liking the way my stuff looks along with hers. I face her again, unbuckling my belt and pulling it from the loops of my jeans, winding the black leather until it's a tight circle that with fit neatly beside my things on her dresser.

I unbutton and unzip my jeans, holding the waistband while I step out of them. I fold them crisply and lay them next to the belt. Finally, I hook my thumbs in the elastic of my black boxer briefs. When I pull them off, my cock springs free, and I hear Evie's gasp, but I can't look at her until I'm done with my ritual or I'll have to start all over, getting it perfect. I fold the underwear once then a second time, placing them next to the jeans, so when it's time to redress, all I'll have to do is follow down the line until my pockets are filled. No scrambling to find a missing shoe, no worry about some chick trying to make off with my fucking hoodie or wallet. If this were anyone besides Evelyn, I'd take the time to go out to her library where I left my shirt to put it line atop her dresser, but her presence is soothing enough to make me not care about it. In fact, the thought of Evie stealing my shirt to wear it and sleep in warms my chest in a way it never has before.

With everything perfectly aligned with an inch of space between each item, I turn to face her, completely unashamed of my nudity. Why would I be? I spend most of my free time honing my body into a machine, trying to achieve perfection with working out, a healthy diet, and by not putting stupid shit into it. It's why I refused to take the meds the doctors tried to prescribe me for my OCD. And if what Evelyn said is true about the lifestyle being enough of a remedy for her own mental health issues, then it makes me wonder if it'll be enough for mine.

"If ever I order you to undress me, this is how I prefer my things," I tell her low, letting it hang in the air that this won't be the only time we'll be together.

"Yes, Mr. Black," she replies, and I can see in her eyes she understands my insinuation. No hesitancy, no pause to think about it, to battle it in her mind. As if she wants there to be more between us as well. And another link in the tightly wound chain inside me loosens.

"Lie in the center of the bed on your back, little mouse."

And she does, and since she follows my order so exquisitely, I'm able to enjoy the image she makes as she climbs gracefully onto her queen-sized bed, atop her perfectly made covers, and centers herself. Her back has barely hit the mattress before I'm there at the foot, my hands on her knees, spreading her legs apart, the only thing covering her the tiny swatch of blue lace barely wide enough to keep her slit hidden.

"Fuck, Evie. Even my fantasies couldn't compare to the reality of you," I murmur, and her face softens.

"Thank you," she says, and an involuntary swallow lets me know her words are heavy with emotion.

Sliding my hands ever so slowly from her knees down the insides of her smooth thighs, I'm fascinated by the immediate goose bumps that lift along her skin, and I glance up to see her nipples are tight, looking almost painfully hard. Her body is so responsive to my barest touch, and it adds to that powerful feeling only she gives me. When my hands reach the middle of her thighs, my grip tightens, my fingers sinking into the softness there, and I spread her open even farther. It causes the lips of her pussy to spread past the tiny underwear, so they only keep just her very center covered. Making it all the more enticing to see what's hidden beneath.

"I have another confession to make, little mouse," I murmur, and I look up from that blue lace to find her breath coming out in quick pants of anticipation.

"Yes, Mr. Black?" she breathes.

"Because of the way I am, because of the control I've always needed but tried to keep hidden, there are things I've never done before. I told you how I've never allowed myself to get rough, worried I'd hurt someone. But there are also things I've never done, because I had no desire to. Finding it repulsive, too intimate to share with someone I cared nothing about." My hands begin to travel the rest of the way down her wide-spread thighs, and they stop just in time to frame her pussy, my thumbs pointing toward the mattress and the rest of my fingers pressing into her mound.

"Th-that's okay. That's one of those hard limits I was t-talking about earlier. It's fine for you to have th-those," she stutters, still trying to be the perfect supportive submissive even as her arousal heightens with anticipation, my hands so close to the epicenter of her lust.

I shake my head slowly then lower my knees to the floor at the foot of her bed. "See, that's the thing." I move suddenly, grasping hold of her legs and yanking her toward me, so her ass rests on the edge of the mattress and her feet have nowhere to go but the tops of my shoulders. "In every one of my fantasies about you, Evelyn, the very first thing I ever wanted to do—" I hook my pointer finger in the lace over her pussy hole, my balls drawing tight at the feel of how soaked it is, for me, because of me, because of her desire... for me. And I pull the blue material to the side, finally revealing my fantasy come to life. "—is taste you," I finish, and with that, I lower my head and take one long, languid swipe of my tongue up her slit, hearing her whimper when I get to her clit. She tastes like ecstasy, the citrusy scent of her skin mixing with the musk of her juices, and it takes everything in me not to come on her floor.

Although I've never eaten a girl out before, I'm not completely inept. I know what and exactly where the clit is and the power it yields. And I know how to kiss like a fucking Casanova. So without even second guessing myself, I let my instincts take over, pull back her little hood with my thumb, and bury my face between her legs, kissing, encircling, licking, sucking, and even nibbling at her clit when she cries out in pleasure, letting me know she likes that.

Suddenly, her hands are buried in my hair. Normally, hands would be promptly removed from anywhere near my head. But for once, I like it. In fact, I fucking love it. I love the way she's tugging me tighter to her, her hips grinding her pussy against my mouth and chin, and when I look up her body, her tits are thrust upward, hiding her face from my position. But when I latch on to her hard little clit, sucking it into my mouth to hold it still so I can lick it with tight circles of my tongue, her back unbows and she lifts her head to look at me. Her eyebrows are furrowed, an almost panicked look on her face, but the pleasure I see in her eyes lets me know not to stop what I'm doing.

"Oh God," she pants and then bites her lush lower lip. I keep my eyes locked with hers, keeping up with the tiny circles, and then I lift my other hand and barely trace her slit with one fingertip. "Oh... oh God." She whimpers, her breaths sharp. "Please."

I don't want to stop what I'm doing, to risk losing the buildup to the very first orgasm I'm giving a woman with my mouth, so I just continue, and I slide just one long digit slowly into her pussy, feeling her inner muscles trying to suck it in deeper.

"Oh God!" she cries. "Please! I need to come. Please let me. Can I please come?" she begs.

And I shudder at the passion in her voice and in her expression. And as I growl a "yes" around her clit, sliding another finger inside her along with the first, her entire body convulses and she lets out the sexiest sound I've ever heard, a moan of relief mixed with the long sob of overwhelming ecstasy. Feeling her pussy clamp onto my fingers, milking them deeper inside her, I have to let go of her panties with my other hand to grip my cock, choking it so I don't come. I can't come. *Don't fucking come yet,* I scream inside my head.

When her hands finally release their tight hold on my hair and she melts into the bed, I slide my fingers out of her gently as I stand. She opens her eyes and looks up at me and shivers when she watches me lick my fingers clean of her juices, my other hand still gripping my cock.

With her looking up at me that way, wonder on her face like she's looking up at a god, as much as I wanted to make this last and learn as much as I could, I can't wait any longer. I have to have her. I have to finally know what her pussy will feel like around my cock.

I let go of my dick and pull her panties down her legs, tossing them into the hamper. I put one knee to the edge of the bed then the other, using my thighs against the inside of hers to push her back up the bed. She's so light, so much smaller than me that it takes only one gentle shove, and then I'm on top of her, bracing myself with my elbows on either side of her head.

"I can't wait any longer to have you, Evelyn," I whisper, and her face softens, and she nods, her eyes locked on mine. "I don't have any condoms. Haven't needed them in months. I've never fucked without one, but I had my physical and all the tests done for swim team, and I'm clean."

Her cheeks flush, and I wonder if it was the reminder that I'm one of her students, but I don't care. I don't fucking care. In this moment, I am a man and she is a woman, and I'll stop at nothing to have her.

"I have to get tested frequently per the rules of the club. I'm clean and on the pill," she replies, and the tension inside me eases a little more.

I lean down and kiss her, absorbing her moan as she tastes herself on my lips and tongue before pulling back enough to look in her eyes. I reach between us and align the head of my rock-hard cock against her soaking wet entrance, and not wanting to disturb this seemingly earth-shattering moment, when the rest of the world has disappeared, I whisper, "Color, little mouse?"

She swallows thickly, but doesn't even blink when she replies, "Green, Mr. Black," and I slowly start to sink into her, even though all I want to do is shove all my steely inches into her at once.

But I can't. I'm not just being some conceited asshole when I say I have a big dick. No. I'm a big guy, and my cock is proportional to the rest of me, and I don't want to hurt her. She may have all sorts of experience, but I heard her gasp when my erection sprang free of my underwear. That was a sound of someone having never seen or been with a man like me. So for this first time, I'm going to ease into her.

At her first whimper when I've barely gotten the head lodged inside her cunt, I pause, opening my eyes when I realize I shut them, trying to concentrate on going slow. Her brows are pulled together, her lips parted as she pants, but there is no look of pain in her eyes. And now that my gaze is locked with hers, all I want to do is watch the emotions play across her face as I sink into her.

I press my hips forward and feel her bring her knees up higher along my sides, spreading herself open farther, trying to accommodate me more like a good little submissive taking my cock. Her little nostrils flare as she takes another inch, breathing through it, adjusting to my girth. I go torturously slow, holding steady, and I watch, fascinated when her head starts to jerk from side to side then press into the mattress beneath her. Her hips begin to rotate, working her sopping wet pussy along my shaft, lubing me up so I sink in even farther.

I feel the sweat break out on my temples, trying to keep control while she writhes beneath me, tempting me, slicing at the reins I hold tightly to. "Hold still," I growl above her, but for the first time, she doesn't follow my order. She shakes her head more forcefully, and it makes me worry my cock is too much for her. So I stop when I'm not even halfway inside her and hiss out a "Color?"

"Green!" she mewls, and before I know what she's doing, she hooks her heels beneath my ass and jerks me forward, forcing me in another couple inches. "Please, Nate. I need you to move."

The use of my nickname is startling, and my brow furrows as she meets my eyes again. "I don't want to hurt you, baby. You're so fucking tight." I call her something I've never called anyone before, finding terms of endearment repulsive and childish, but it just slips out. I want to take care of her, keep her safe, not bring her any pain, and it just fell from my lips so naturally.

Her frantic movements still when she hears it, and she melts beneath me, her entire body going lax and making me sink another inch inside. She lifts her hands slowly, as if readying herself if I order her not to, and places her gentle fingers to my jaw. When I don't move or flinch away, she slides her fingertips upward until her palms cup my cheeks, and she looks deep into my eyes, saying all sorts of sweet nothings and meaningful confessions without even uttering a word. And then her hands move farther and into my hair until she grasps the back of my head and pulls me toward her. I let her overpower me, let her tug me near, and when my face nuzzles into her neck, breathing in her citrusy, clean scent, she turns her head so she can whisper in my ear.

"I'm yours, Mr. Black. I can handle it. Let go and take from me what you want."

And with that, without even questioning it, my muscles stiffen, my thighs tense, I link my arms beneath her and grip onto her shoulders, and with one powerful thrust, I shove all my thick inches into her, hearing her cry out as the head of me slams into her cervix. Her walls grip me tighter than a fist, and I choke out "Color?" one last time to be sure, and when she wails, "Green, oh God, yes, green!" That's all it takes for me to finally toss the reins farther away from my grip than they've ever been before, and I pull back so only the tip of me is still lodged in her cunt before I power my way back inside.

With a growl, I shoot up to my knees and circle my hands around her hips to grip her ass, holding her lower half up and steady as her shoulders press in the bed. Her arms fall above her head, and her hands grip her pillow, and I watch my fantasies come to life as I start to thrust in and out of her tight, wet heat. I glance away from her beautiful face to watch her tits bounce with every plunge of my cock. And then my eyes trail farther to watch our connection, the image obscene with how far her cunt is stretched to take my girth. Her pussy lips are red and glistening with her juices, and with each outstroke, I see how shiny she's made my dick, her natural lube making it easy for me to pound into her.

Her cries of pleasure fill her room along with my grunts of desire. My fingers dig into her ass, the muscles of my arms bulging as I keep her held steady while I fuck into her, my hips creating the perfect movements to cause my cock to drag along the top wall of her pussy with every pull out, my shaft stroking along her clit with every stroke in.

Sweat drips along my hairline and down my back and chest, but for once it's because of exertion instead of trying to keep a hold of my control. Everything is heightened, and each drop of sweat feels like a fingertip caressing my body as they fall along my skin.

"Yes!" Evie mewls after a particularly rough thrust, and it spurs me on. I drop her hips and fall forward, my hands on either side of her head. She meets my stare, and when I see her lips tilt upward in a little smile as I continue to pound into her, it does something to me, loosens more of those chain links inside me enough that I give into another one of my fantasies.

In one fluid movement, because she's so light I can just put her where I want her, I pull out and flip her over, enjoying her little disappointed whimper at the loss of me inside her. But she doesn't have to be disappointed for long, because I kick her knees apart with my own and thrust inside her from behind, no hesitation, no going slow, no warning, the way I've always wanted to fuck but never allowed myself to. And I glance up, catching movement, and realize we're now facing her closet doors that are made of mirrors, and I see the look of pure ecstasy on Evie's face when I give in to my own desires.

I grip her soft hips in my big hands, and I look away from the mirror long enough to watch my cock disappear inside her, seeing more of Evelyn Richards than I ever even dared to dream of. My hands grip her in a way that spreads her ass cheeks, and I see the little hole centered between them. My nostrils flare at the dirty thoughts the sight sparks in my mind, and since she's still distracted by the steady pistoning of my cock in and out of her, she pays no mind as one hand leaves her hip.

It's not until I reach beneath her to gather some of her wetness and bring it back up to circle that little hole that she takes notice, and her entire body stiffens. I meet her eyes in the mirror, my pace slowing slightly so I can get an honest answer out of her when I ask, "Color, little mouse?"

"Um…" She moans as my cock slides along her G-spot. I circle her asshole with my fingertip again. "I, uh…. Yellow."

I nod, bending to place a kiss between her shoulder blades. "Another time then," I murmur against her soft flesh, and when I sit back up on my knees, I see her nod.

I pick up my pace again, and soon, I'm on the brink, and with Evie's cries of pleasure becoming louder, one starting before the previous ends, I know she's close too.

"I don't want to come like this," I say, more to myself than to her, as I pull out and flip her once more to her back. "I want to look into your eyes when I make you come on my cock."

And as if my words have a physical effect on her, she does exactly that with only three more powerful thrust of my hips. "Oh my God," she exhales, her nails digging into my back, and that's all it takes to make me follow her over the edge.

Her pussy milks me, her inner walls fluttering around me as I plant myself deep and growl ferociously, while the most powerful, soul-shattering, mind-altering orgasm takes over my entire body. I've never felt anything like it before, not with another person, not even with my hand while fantasies of Ms. Richards played through my mind. Nothing could ever compare to the reality of actually coming inside her after being allowed to give in to the urges within me.

The aftershocks seem to go on forever, and the way her body continues to twitch and shudder tells me it's the same for her. But the look on her face and how tiny her body feels beneath me, all I want to do is wrap her up and take care of her, to soothe her after what we just experienced together, not giving a damn about my own feelings.

I pull out of her, being as gentle as possible, and I can't help the smile that pulls at my lips at her little frown when she loses my cock. In a fluid series of movements, my back is propped against her cushioned headboard and I've gathered her in my lap. I curl her against my chest, pulling my knees up to keep her locked in place. I run on instinct alone, running my fingers through her hair, gently stroking her soft skin, absorbing the closeness it brings.

And I realize, in this moment, I've never felt so powerful. Not when I teased her and made her cower. Not when I blackmailed her, making her think I'd reveal her secrets. Not even when I made her come with my mouth and then my cock. No. I have never felt more powerful than I do right this second, with Evelyn curled up and relaxed against my chest, completely surrendered, completely trusting, and fully at peace while I bring her gently back to the here and now.

She might've made it sound like aftercare was just for the submissive's benefit, and maybe that's all she believes it's for. But it seems she has a thing or two still to learn, because this feels like pure bliss for this Dominant in training.

CHAPTER 9

Evie

I'm floating, hovering over my body, seeing from above as Nathaniel holds me to his chest, soothing me, petting me, whispering sweet things at the top of my head before planting kisses on my hair every few words. I smile down at the picture we make. I look so tiny in his arms, this overgrown man cradling me after he just delivered two of the best orgasms I've ever had, and certainly the best sex of my life.

It wasn't even particularly creative, when compared to the things that go on at Club Alias. There were no toys or devices, no role playing, no costumes or power plays. No games. It was just a powerful man who craves control and a willing woman who wanted to give it to him, and he worked my body like he created it, like he knew it from the inside out. And now he does.

I don't want to leave this cocoon of happiness he's surrounded me in. Wasn't it just a couple hours ago when I was sitting in my car, super bitter that he'd ruined my night of getting my fix of this? I almost laugh, thinking about how nothing any of the Doms at the club could have done would've held a candle to what I feel right now. I bet this high will last far longer than a week. But at the same time, I don't think I want to wait even that long to get my next dose of Nate Black.

I see him tilt my head back and look deep into my eyes, but I can't hear what he's saying. I'm not in there, my consciousness still floating just above us. Yet I take notice when his face starts to look worried. I see myself blink at him, a smile curling just the corners of my lips, but that does little to sooth his furrowed brow and the way his biceps are starting to bunch as he holds me tighter.

I sigh, knowing I should go back, knowing I should soothe him, since he's never experience this before. I should tell him how proud I am to have been his first sub, how amazing it is that his instincts told him exactly what to do concerning aftercare, since I hadn't really explained thoroughly how to do it after I told him what it was.

With one last moment hovering above our bodies, I take a mental snapshot to keep inside my mind and heart forever, and I know this image will be the one I compare every experience moving forward to.

Back in my body, I blink several times and take a cleansing breath in then out, relaxing even further against Nathaniel's expansive chest.

"Evie, please say something. Are you all—"

I purr against him. "Never better," I whisper, wanting him to go back to the softly murmured words against my hair.

"Fuck, you scared me. I thought... I thought I'd been too rough and—"

"Shhh," I soothe, not caring that I'm essentially shushing my Dom. But he needs the assurance. He needs to know he did nothing wrong. "Subspace."

His biceps relax, and it makes me sink away from him a little as he peers down at me, surprise covering his face. "Subspace? I... I got you to subspace? Without even anything... special?" he asks, his eyes looking back and forth between mine, and I smile.

"But it was special, Mr. Black." I try to lift my arm to boop him on the nose, but the limb is too heavy. "*You're* special."

He must see the sincerity in my eyes, because a boyish smile spreads across his face, making him look younger than what his very manly body was just capable of doing to me. "You're special to me too, Evelyn," he murmurs, and then he lifts me halfway to meet his lowering face, and he kisses me with such sweetness it does something funny to my heart.

Never have I felt anything I've ever done as a submissive in my heart before. The satisfaction it gives me is always felt in my gut... while it quiets my anxious mind... experiencing the pleasure throughout my body, and maybe a little in my soul, just knowing I've finally discovered who I am meant to be. But I've never felt any of it in my heart before. Not until this man holding me looked into my eyes and asked for my help. Not until he told me to my face that he thought I was the most beautiful woman he'd ever seen. And not until this man kissed me like his life depended on it.

Suddenly, I'm moving, and Nathaniel standing up with me still cradled in his arms brings me out of my thoughts. I give in to it, enjoying not having to use any brainpower, continuing to submit myself to his whims as he does with me what he pleases.

"Let's get cleaned up, shall we?" he murmurs as he enters the bathroom and flips on the light. He's not asking me, not forcing me to make a decision. He's just talking out loud in that deliciously deep voice of his, and I nuzzle against him. He sits on the side of my huge tub, the first upgrade I ever made to my house, since the one that was in here when I bought the place was tiny and rusted. This one is a giant garden tub with jets, and he perches me on his lap, one arm still around me as he uses the other to turn on the faucet and get the temperature to his liking.

While the tub fills, he just holds me, rubbing his big calloused hand up and down my naked back, lulling me deeper into my tranquil state. I feel boneless, more relaxed than I've ever felt in my life, and the only thing I'm super aware of is how wonderful his cologne smells where my face is buried in his neck.

I don't even realize the words are out of my mouth—"God, you smell good. You always smell sooo good"—until I feel the rumble of his chuckle inside his chest.

"Oh yeah?" he prompts, kissing my cheek with the corner of his lips, since my face is still buried in the crook of his neck.

In this peaceful level of consciousness, I don't even blush. I'm not embarrassed by what he heard me say. "Yep." I pop the P. "Whenever you leave the library, there's always this faint little hint of it left behind, and it always makes me wet."

His naked cock beneath my thighs jerks, and I smile when he growls a startled, "Fuck." It doesn't make me flinch this time. I don't think anything would make me flinch right now, not in this hazy state of bliss I'm still in. "Guess I'll be buying stock in Aqua de Fuckboy next time I speak to my financial advisor."

That makes me giggle. "You have a financial advisor? What's an eighteen-year-old need with a financial advisor?"

"When I turned eighteen, all my trust funds hit. I'm not one to just... hit the lottery and go buy mansions around the world and cars to fill a warehouse. That would be fucking stupid," he says quietly, and for some reason, that brings me back to reality a little more, but in a good way. It makes me admire him even more, this man I knew was brilliant at school, but now know he's also smart when it comes to real life.

I pull my face out of his neck and meet his eyes. "I did the same when my parents died," I confess, and his eyes soften, but not with pity. I can see clearly the softness comes from me divulging something about my personal life to him he didn't know.

"My parents are still alive. My trusts came from older generations," he explains, and I sink back against him.

I peek over his shoulder to see the water is only halfway done, the one bad thing about having such a big tub—it takes forever to fill. But I'm enjoying getting to know more about Nate. There seems to be so much more to him than the man who's intimidated the hell out of me since the day I met him.

"What are your parents like? I don't think I've ever met them at school before," I ask, and he starts back up rubbing my back.

"I got lucky. My parents are actually cool as fuck. My mom is sweet and one of those Pinterest moms, even though she could just pay someone to do everything for her. She wants to do it herself. My dad works a lot, but when he's home, he's actually present. He's a great dad. Like I said, lucky," he tells me, and it surprises me. I always pictured the parents of Nathaniel Black IV to be the uptight snobbish type, the stereotypical people always portrayed in movies and shows who own things like towns and freaking private academies.

He must sense my shock, because he chuckles again. "Right? I think my dad was just hellbent on being nothing like the Black men before him. And he married for love, not status like the generations before him."

That makes me smile. "That's... interesting. I imagined.... I don't know. It surprised me more, because of... how you are," I say gently.

"My OCD, you mean?" he asks, but there's no defensiveness in his tone.

"Yeah."

"Mine is the hereditary kind, not trauma-induced," he replies, and I meet his eyes once more. "Yeah, I've been diagnosed. I've seen therapists and psychiatrists about it."

My brow furrows. "Then... why—"

"Don't I have it under control with medication?" he finishes my question, and I nod. "Same as you, little mouse. Never found the right cocktail, and the ones that did help, I didn't like the way they made my body feel. I felt like I was putting poison in my body, and I don't know if you noticed, but I take a little bit of pride in this body." He grins.

"Oh, I noticed," I murmur, looking down at his deliciously masculine chest before biting my bottom lip, and I can't help but giggle when his cock twitches beneath me again.

"God, that giggle. I swear, when I heard it the first time when I was listening to you at the club—"

"Spying on me, you mean?" I lift a brow.

"Tomatoes, to-mah-toes." He winks. "I swear the sound of it did something to my chest. Like it tightened and loosened at the same time. It made me feel guilty that I'd spent all these months picking on you instead of trying to make you laugh."

The confession comes so easily from his lips that I don't even know how to respond, so I stay quiet, and soon he leans us over to turn off the water, and I hear him splash a little to test the temperature.

"Perfect," he murmurs, and he stands so suddenly that I squeak and wrap my arms around his neck. "Little mouse." He laughs low. "Like I'd let you fall." He shakes his head, and he steps into the tub and lowers us into the water. Without making me think about it, he spins me around how he wants me, between his legs and leaning back against his chest. "How do I turn on the jets?" he asks, and I point to the button in one corner of the tub, loving that he didn't ask me if I want them on, not forcing me to make a decision, just asking how to get what he wants.

Before he pushes it though, he picks up my citrus body wash from several bottles I have on the edge and holds it up to read the label. I smile when he pops it open and brings it to his nose, giving it two audible sniffs. "Mmm, this is what you wore tonight," he says, more to himself than to me, and then I giggle again when he tells me, "This is my favorite part." I watch curiously as he turns the bottle upside down and squeezes a figure-8 of green soap around my breasts, making me squeal at the cold liquid, but I don't move, wanting to see what he does next. And then he pushes the button to turn on the jets, and I grin in delight as he laughs boyishly when the tub quickly fills with a thick cloud of bubbles.

He kicks his legs a little when the bubbles get too high, and it dissipates them enough that they're not in my face. We relax in the jets for a few quiet minutes, taking in the simple pleasure, and then he reaches behind him and pushes the button again to turn them off, and immediately the bubbles start to pop all around us. I close my eyes as I rest my head back somewhere between his shoulder and chest and feel his arms come around me. Using only his big, calloused hands, he begins to rub his palms along my body starting with my biceps and working all the way down my arms until he momentarily laces his fingers with mine before working back up again. Then he moves inward to my breasts, massaging them gently, and I glance down to see they look so much smaller when giant hands are on them. But he doesn't seem to mind, seeing as his cock hardens behind me.

He takes a split second to reach between our bodies to adjust his erection so it lies straight up to his belly button. He picks up where he left off, caressing my breast before rolling my nipples between his thumbs and the knuckles of his pointer fingers, and I gasp and arch my back to get closer to his hands. But he lets go of them and continues his massage downward over my ribs then farther to dip into my belly button, making me twitch. His long, muscled arms reach farther, until he cups my center, and I hold my breath, wondering what he'll do.

Now that I've come fully back into my body, I feel the soreness between my legs. He must feel how swollen I am, how wonderfully used my pussy feels after what he did to me, because his touch is gentle as he presses the V of his first two fingers on either side of my slit, massaging them up and down my lower lips.

I purr as I melt against him, letting my legs fall wider apart over his. I feel the slickness as he dips his fingers into my pussy, trying to hold still as he rubs carefully, cleaning away his cum and my juices. He moves then, and I'm in such a trance I don't realize I'm trapped until his legs hook over mine. It's then I feel his other arm has come around the front of me to hold down my arms, so now my legs are locked open and I can't move my upper body.

I'm at his mercy, and he's got a free hand and an obscenely long reach.

CHAPTER 10

Evie

With my breath starting to come in pants, my heart starts to pound, never having been aroused again so closely after coming out of aftercare. But like the good Dominant Nathaniel is turning out to naturally be, he senses my change in emotion and asks, "Color, little mouse?" against my ear from behind. His breath sends a shiver down my body, tightening my nipples even further.

"Um... green. Just... unexpected. I'm... I'm okay." I nod.

"Very good," he rumbles low, and he continues where he left off, toying with my pussy. He plays with my clit with the pads of two fingers, making fire spread from my core outward. I can barely move an inch, and only my hips, and I press my head back against him, turning my face so my forehead presses against his jaw.

He dips a finger inside me, and his cock jerks where it's pressed between us, and I clench around him, making him groan. "Do you know how fucking hot it is to know I'm using my cum inside you as lube?" he asks, and he curls his finger to drag it along that special place on my inner wall.

I shudder. "Yes, Mr. Black," I whisper, my legs straining against his even though they're no match for the long, thick muscles that are barely even flexed to keep me trapped. My toes curl at the delicious feelings his fingers are providing.

He circles my clit, building... building... building me up, and when my breaths become pants, he eases his fingers into me once again, toying with me, taking me to the brink and then pulling me back. I want to whine, to beg, to complain that he's not giving me what I want, but that's not how this works. He is my Master right now, and he'll give me what he pleases. And right now, what pleases him is playing my body like a savant.

Back and forth, he strums the chords of my desire, circling, circling, circling my clit then dipping his fingers in to stroke along my G-spot. Circling, circling, circling, then back inside, lulling me until I pick up on the rhythm and the number, and I realize he must be counting in his head, turning my pleasure into a ritual. I don't know whether to try to stop it or not. Should I let him add something else to his list of compulsions, or is it inevitable? And before I can worry any more about it, his finger is on my clit once more, circling... circling... circling... but instead of dipping into my pussy, his fingers go lower, finding my back hole and tracing along the rim.

My thighs convulse, instinctively trying to close, but his legs hold tight, his arm squeezing tighter around me. And this time, he doesn't ask me what color I'm at. He simply breathes, "Relax, little mouse."

"But... I've never let anyone do any type of anal play before," I say in one exhale, and he groans, his chest vibrating against my back.

"Something that'll be all mine then," he murmurs to himself. Then to me, he whispers, "Trust me to take care of you and know how far to take you."

And I don't know if it's the smartest decision of my life, to give in to an untrained Dominant, to allow him to do something to me that has always been a soft limit for me, something I was wary of but not quite completely off the table. But for some reason, I do trust him. And I do want to be a good submissive and give him what he wants. So I do as he ordered and relax, forcing myself to melt against him and let the tension leave my legs.

"That's my girl," he murmurs, and my heart beams inside my chest, making me feel like I'm glowing all over under his praise and being called his.

He goes back to circling my clit, the same number as before, and again he slides his fingers past my pussy to press against my anus, dipping one finger just inside.

"I'm going to let go of your arms so I can use my other hand now. Do not move," he commands, and it makes me relax even more, trust him even further, because he has knowledge I had been afraid he didn't have. But of course he does—he's brilliant Nathaniel Black. Why *wouldn't* he know you shouldn't touch a woman's pussy with something that's been in her ass?

With one fingertip of his right hand still pressed inside my hole, his left slides sensually over my curves, making me arch like a cat in heat, as he makes his way down to start circling my clit, and I moan at the feel of everything happening at once, no longer able to focus on just one sensation at a time.

"That's it, baby," he whispers, and I melt further against him at the name. "Feel my fingers strumming this pretty little clit. Focus all your attention there, and what I do to your tight little ass will only heighten your pleasure." He says it in a way like he knows it for a fact, and I decide to listen to him, allowing the student to become the teacher. Since I've never let anyone do any of this before, I wouldn't know, but it truly feels like he knows what he's doing. So I give in, sinking back into my role as submissive, and let my Master have his way, because I always have my safe word just in case.

Doing as he said, I let my mind zero in on my clit as he picks up the circles from before, breathing through it as I vaguely feel his digit in my ass begin to massage my rim. I have to focus on other things as well—his masculine sighs behind me, the way he rocks his hardness so subtly against my back, the flexing of his calves over mine, how sexy his sinewy, tan forearms look against my much lighter stomach—because if I focus too fully on my clit, I'm going to come too quickly.

When I allow my focus to fall back to my center, I realize he's worked his finger in farther, and I suck in a breath.

"Evelyyyn," Nathaniel singsongs, and I whimper. "You're not doing what I asked, are you? You tightened up."

"I'm... sorry. It's overwhelming. If I focus on my clit, I'll come too fast," I reply.

He chuckles behind me. "Who ever told you there's such a thing as coming too fast?" I think it might be a rhetorical question until he prompts, "What do you think will happen if you come?"

"That you... you'll stop. And then you won't get to do what you wanted to do, and I will have ruined it for you," I breathe, as he continues his circles on my clit.

He shakes his head. "Baby, if you come, I'll just keep going. I'll keep going, even if you beg me to stop. The only thing that's going to make me end this is if you call your safe word. Your orgasms are my reward. They don't tell me to stop. They tell me, 'Good job, keep going.'"

His words make me shudder, and I want to cry at how different, how amazing he is. Every other Dom I've been with has liked to withhold completion, except for the one with the Hitachi, who gets off on seeing just how many times he can make a woman come before she loses consciousness. But Nathaniel... he's wanting to give me as much pleasure as my body can take. I don't have to ask his permission to come. As many things as he wants to control, that's apparently not one of them, calling the ability to get me off a "reward."

"Now, focus on your clit, and when you're ready, I want you push out with your asshole. It'll open that ring of muscles, and I'll be able to slide in without hurting you. Trust me," he says, and I nod against him.

My mind's eye zeroes in on my clit, and that fire starts to build once more, spreading through my core and down my legs, and I moan at how good it feels, and then I give him what he wants and flex my anus. He feels the tightness around his finger loosen, because he slides his long finger all the way into me without nearly as much resistance, and I gasp at the intrusion.

He picks up the speed of his circles, murmuring against my face, "Very good, little mouse," and I'm shocked at how good it feels. My hips start to grind involuntarily, and that fire in my core starts to build and build as he moves his finger inside me.

I don't know where to focus anymore, since what he's doing to my ass actually feels wonderful, so I don't need to distract myself from it any longer. But fuck, what he's doing to my clit his exquisite, so I try to take everything in all at once. And before I know what's happening, an orgasm slams into me, and I arch against him, his finger going deeper, the others working my clit faster, and my voice is echoing, echoing off the walls as I beg him for more. And he wastes no time giving it to me.

The next thing I know I'm on my knees with Nathaniel behind me, and he's pressing between my shoulder blades until my face is lying on the wide edge of the tub. My arms come up to help me hold on.

"That little cunt feel empty?" he growls, his hand no longer on my clit but the other still at my ass, with the aftershocks of my orgasm still shooting through my body, I let out a mewl when suddenly he starts to add a second finger.

"Oh God," I whimper, breathing out as I push my inner muscle outward to make it easier for its entrance.

His other hand comes down on my ass cheek, the sting reverberating through my lower half and making me moan. "Mmm, you like that, little mouse?" His hand comes down on the other cheek, somehow instinctively knowing to mix it up, and I pant his name over and over as he continues to work his fingers inside me. "I asked you a question. Does. That little cunt. Feel. Empty?" he repeats, this time spanking me between each word, the sound obscene since my ass and his hand is still wet with bathwater.

"Yes!" I call. "Yes, I feel so empty without you inside me, Mr. Black."

He bends over me, his hot breath sending a shiver down my spine, when he asks, "Who?"

"Mr. Black," I whimper as he pulls his fingers out then shoves them back into my ass, the ring of muscle now loosened enough to accommodate the movement.

"Try again," he growls, twisting his digits and scissoring them inside me, making me curse.

"Nathaniel," I whine, shuddering at the rumble of his chuckle against my back.

I feel him shake his head as he adds a third finger, and I feel tears prickle my eyes at the stretch. But it doesn't hurt enough to call my safe word. I know from the past two fingers I just need to give myself a chance to get used to it.

"Mmm, as much as I love hearing my name on your lips while I finger fuck your tight little virgin ass, that's not the direction I'm looking for. I'll give you one last chance. Who?" His voice is deliciously devious. I can hear the dark smile in his tone, the wickedness. I can picture it so clearly in my mind, because it's the tone he's always used on me at school, and my pussy clenches, begging for something, anything to fill it.

"Please," I beg, and I try one last name, praying it's what he's asking for so I can get my reward. "Yes, I feel so empty without you inside me..., Master."

And as soon as the word leave my lips, I hear his growl of pleasure, and I scream with relieved ecstasy as he slams his cock inside me without warning. One perfect thrust home, filling my pussy completely, his fingers still inside me, and I come so hard and so suddenly that I nearly lose my grip on the side of the tub. But he's right there, holding me up, keeping me steady as he starts to move in and out of me, albeit more shallowly than he did on my bed, because his hand his still between us, massaging the inside of my ass, keeping my muscles loose, and I know... I just know... he's not done with me.

"Fuck, I love when you come on my dick," he pants behind me as he continues to thrust, and I can't even respond. I have no words as he makes me feel things I've never felt before. "You're so wet. Soaking me. I can feel your come dripping down my balls you're so fucking drenched."

My face flames at his vulgar words, at the mention of how wet I am.

"It's so good, baby. So fucking good," he praises, and my muscles relax taking him deeper, easier, feeling my desire build once again. But then he pulls out of me, his cock out of my pussy and his fingers leaving my ass, and I feel empty once again, exposed, vulnerable. Until I feel the head of his cock at my back hole, and I shut my eyes tightly.

"Don't be scared, little mouse. I'm going to make it so good for you. And once you feel what it's like to have my cock inside your tight little ass, you'll beg for it in the future." His words are a dark promise, and he says it so confidently I believe him, giving in to the possibility instead of calling my safe word.

I'm vaguely aware of him pulling back enough to stroke his tip, and when he presses it back against me, it feels wetter, so I know he must've lubed himself up more with his saliva. Such a good Dom, taking the time to do everything he can to make this a good experience.

"On this night—" He starts to add pressure against my hole, and I remember to do what he said, pushing outward with my muscles. "—I gave you the real me. You're the first and only woman to accept the part of me I've always kept hidden." He slides in an inch, and with the head of his cock now lodged inside my ass, he lets go of his shaft and brings it around the front of my hips to start circling my clit once more. It's oversensitive from all the attention, but I know I'm going to need the distraction, because his cock is so... much... more than even his three long, thick fingers. "In a way, I gave you my virginity, because it was the first time the real me was ever allowed to come forth and make love."

My breath catches at the use of those words, because up until now, he'd always described the intercourse he had as sex, or fucking. And my muscles go soft, allowing him to sink another inch deeper.

"And now, you're letting me take your virgin ass, sweet, beautiful Evelyn," he whispers low, his words so sincere, even with their vulgarity, that they bring tears to my eyes.

Added to the overwhelming sensations running rampant through my body, the tears start to come in a steady stream, falling over the bridge of my nose and into my hairline with my face turned to the side, pressing to the edge of the tub. He pushes in another inch, and he can't see my tears, but he must hear my sniffle, because he stops, his finger pausing.

Before he can even ask, I speak before being spoken to, my words heartfelt and strong. "Don't stop, Nate. Please. Don't stop. I feel it too, and I'm all yours."

And without questioning me, I feel him shudder, and then he leans forward, sinking his fingers into my pussy at the same time he glides all the way into my ass.

"Oh... God!" I cry and feel the heel of his palm clamp down on my mound, keeping his fingers steady, deep in my front hole as he starts to slowly slide in and out of my back one. Every time his hips piston into my ass, it vibrates his hand, the pressure on my clit just enough that I feel everything start to build once again.

With tears still steadily streaming out of my eyes, I give in to all the sensations, and soon, I'm coming... coming so hard I let out a silent scream as I just take it, take everything he has to give me. And when one orgasm ends, another one immediately begins, until more are rolling in one on top of the other, giving me multiples like waves of an ocean.

The water laps roughly at our thighs with his pounding movements back and forth, but I don't care if it soaks my entire floor. Nothing matters. Nothing. Except for where Nate and I are connected in more than one way, and more than just physically. And I know after this I'll never be the same. After this, I'll be ruined for anyone else.

CHAPTER 11

Nate

I've never felt such bliss. Nothing could compare to this. And I'm not just talking about fucking Evelyn's virgin ass. While there is nothing that will ever feel like being buried deep in that forbidden place, somewhere no other man has ever been before, I mean her complete surrender. Her complete and total submission. And when she told me *"I'm all yours,"* it was all I could do not to come right then and there, without even being all the way inside her, without even having taken that first stroke of my cock in her ass.

But then she started to come, and the sounds she made, and the feel of her muscles surrounding me was an addictive feeling I didn't want to end. I become obsessed with it, counting the times I make her come over and over again. And I promise I'll stop. I promise I'll give in if she calls her safe word, or if I feel like she truly can't take anymore. But until then, I keep counting my thrusts, counting how many it takes each time to get her off.

But then her orgasms start multiply and combine in a way I can't tell when one ends and another begins, and I lose count, lose track of all my numbers, and for the first time in my life... I don't care. Not one fuck is given. I don't have the compulsion to start over. I don't have the clawing need for order and symmetry. I just give in to the feel of my cock in her ass, my fingers in her pussy, my palm clamped down on that sweet little cunt, and when I tune into the fact that it's my name she's chanting over and over like a prayer—my dream girl, my fantasy come to life—I bury myself to the hilt and roar as I come, filling her ass with jet after jet of my cum, until I collapse atop her back. But even spent, I make sure not to give her all my weight, my tiny little mouse. As much as everything in me wants to just roll over and die with happiness, it's the need to take care of my woman that overpowers everything else.

I reach down and pull the plug, and the water starts draining quickly. I carefully, ever so gently start backing out of her, and I know she's back in that special place of blissful nothingness, subspace, because not a single muscle in her tenses, not even a flinch. Cautiously, I pick her up, looking up and around for a moment, seeing the shower is separate from her tub, and I step out with her in my arms and carry her into the much smaller space, pulling the glass door behind us and closing us in.

I look down into her face. Her eyes are open but vacant, and it would be eerie if there wasn't a small smile on her lips. She looks blitzed out of her mind, and my chest practically puffs up knowing I was the one who did that to her.

"I need to wash us off again, baby. So I need you to stand up, okay?" I ask, but unlike every other time I've asked her to do something, she doesn't jump to attention without hesitation.

Hoping she'll be able to stand at least enough so I can hold her with only one arm, I lower her feet to the ground, breathing out a sigh of relief when I see her knees lock. She leans against me, her face nestling into my chest as I wrap my arm around her and hold her to me. I turn the showerhead away from us and twist on the water, and when it's warm, I take it off the hook and spray us down. It takes some finagling, but I'm able to pour some body wash into my hand and use it to gently clean between her legs, quickly rinsing it off when I hear her intake of breath as if it stings. When the soap is off of her, she sighs, comfortable once again. I make quick work of cleaning and rinsing my cock, not bothering with the rest of me, and then shut off the water. I push open the door with one hand then pick her up once more, grabbing the two towels off the rack on my way out of the bathroom and carrying her straight to the bed.

I sit her on the foot of the mattress, wrapping one of the towels around her so she doesn't get cold and using the other to dry off the rest of her body. When I'm done with her legs, I wrap the second one around my hips and finish drying her upper half. I grip the towel in my hand, my obsession with order and tidiness warring with my need to stay with her. The first half wants to go back into the bathroom and hang up the damn towel, but the Dom in me refuses to leave my sub like this.

Eventually, the Dom wins, and I toss the wet towel into her hamper, promising myself I'll throw all of it into her washer before I leave, like a fucking gentleman.

I unhook my towel from around my hips and dry myself quickly, throwing it into the hamper, and then I pick Evie up and carry her to the head of her bed. I pull back the covers, knocking the decorative pillows that hadn't fallen off during our first time together onto the floor.

I lay us down in the center of the bed, turning her so my front is flush with her back, even our legs locking together like jigsaw pieces. As I wrap my arm around her front and lace my fingers with hers, I feel her tug our hands toward her body until they're nestled between her breasts. And with wet towels in her hamper and pillows strewn on the floor, with my shirt in another room instead of in line with everything else on her dresser and wet footprints along the bathroom floor, it's then I realize... Evelyn is my dose, my drug, the perfect cocktail, and I'm exactly where I need to be.

CHAPTER 12

Evie

I've heard about those weighted blankets; I think it was in a Facebook ad while I was scrolling or something. Thousands of reviews saying how wonderful they were, how it was the best sleep they'd ever gotten in their life. Things like "great for anxiety!" and "perfect for people with RLS!" But I just never actually clicked the Buy button. One of those, meh, maybe later type of things.

As I come awake Saturday morning, my first thought is, *Did I finally click the Buy button and just forgot about it?* Because one, the weight pushing down on me feels wonderful and cozy, like I'm swaddled in warmth and being hugged, and two, I just had the best night of sleep ever. I don't think I even rolled over in the night, when usually I toss and turn constantly. I once tracked my sleep with my Apple Watch, and the results were... laughable and depressing at the same time. The only time I even *reach* REM sleep is on Friday nights after my time at Club Alias.

But then my "blanket" moves, rocking its lower half against my ass, and I think, *Damn, my blanket has some serious morning wood*, and the night before appears clearly in my mind and my eyes pop open.

The first thing I see is my bathroom door is open, since that's what's directly in front of my line of sight. Another clear sign I slept soundly and hard. I usually can't sleep with my bathroom door open; it freaks me out, thinking something is going to come out of the mirror and kill me. As I tilt my chin down, the second thing I see is that Nathaniel Black IV's clothing and other belongings are, in fact, still perfectly lined up on my dresser.

So it wasn't a dream. The memories of last night swirling through my head weren't just a delicious wet dream. Obviously not, unless I got really freaking creative and rough with my dildo, seeing as—when I focus my attention on assessing my body—my ladybits and my *ass* are sore.

My ass... is sore. My ass is sore, because not only did I have sex with Nathaniel Black IV, but I also let him dominate me and tried anal play for the first time. And not only had I tried anal play for the first time, but had I just let him use a finger or two? Maybe a little butt plug? *No!* I had full-on anal sex... with Nathaniel Black *the fucking fourth!*

"You're thinking too loud," the student in question murmurs behind me, pulling me closer and pressing his erection against my sore ass again.

I swallow, but somehow, my building freak-out seems to lessen, or at least comes to a standstill. In fact, I almost smile at his words, remembering last night and how he seemed to be so in tune with me.

A few more bits and pieces come to light, him taking care of me when we were all finished, my limbs being too heavy to move. I couldn't even formulate the words to thank him, having never been that far gone into subspace. Not even when Midas used the Hitachi and I got six orgasms, one after another. Last night was on a whole new level, and I doubt I'll ever experience anything like it again.

"If ever I order you to undress me, this is how I prefer my things."

His words from last night come back to me, making me feel equal parts nervous about what the future holds and comfort that he'd want to be with me again. Which is ridiculous. This shouldn't happen again. This shouldn't have happened in the first place. He's my student!

He's a consenting adult.

I work for his family!

No one has to know.

He... he's made my life a living panic attack since the first day of school!

He felt something for you he didn't understand, didn't know how to deal with.

"I haven't been with anyone else since that first time I fucked you inside my mind, because I knew it was pointless. No one could measure up to you, Evelyn."

Nathaniel growls behind and above my head, and suddenly I'm on my back and he's on top of me, looking down into my face. "I can hear you warring with yourself, and you haven't even spoken a word, little mouse." His hair is sexy as hell, coming forward over one eye. It makes me clench, and I flinch at the ache inside. He must see my discomfort on my face, because his sleepy scowl clears and his eyes soften. "Am I hurting you?" he asks, lifting some of his weight off of me.

My face flushes, which is stupid after the night we had. "N-No. I'm just... a little sore," I whisper the last part, and his face softens even more.

And then he's kissing me, sweet and slow, and I whimper at how tender he can be, when he'd shown me anything but before last night. He tosses back the covers, and I realize then we are both naked, something else that shows I slept like the dead last night. Normally, I have to at least wear panties, because I can't sleep feeling so vulnerable and exposed.

He kisses down my body, and I'm so stunned after waking up in Nate's arms that I just let it happen, the sub in me stretching her arms above her head and then settling in, loving that she's not being locked away after a Friday adventure.

Nathaniel fits his shoulders between my legs, gently spreading me open, and then he's there, just looking at me, staring at my most secret place. I watch him, unable to move because he didn't tell me I can, but as he continues looking at me there, open and on full display for his perusal, my breath starts to come out in pants as I try to control my anxiousness. *What is he staring at? Does he think I'm ugly down there? Is it all swollen and gross-looking from having been ravaged and fucked?*

But then I sink into my pillows, relieved when he murmurs, "So fucking beautiful," before he leans closer, pressing his nose to my mound and inhaling deeply. My heart thuds at the tenderness in his voice, especially knowing he'd never gone down on anyone before last night, because he found it too intimate. "And you smell so good, so... intoxicating," he adds, and I shudder as his hot breath tickles my over-sensitive flesh. And as if he knows exactly what to do, he lays his tongue flat along my slit and drags it upward oh-so-slowly, and with a gentleness that brings tears to my eyes.

I moan at how soothing it feels, melting into the bed, my legs going lax, making my knees fall all the way open.

"Feel good, baby?" he whispers against me, as if needing to be assured what he's doing is right.

"Yesss," I say on an exhale while he laps languidly at my inner lips, whimpering when he dips carefully inside.

And then his hands are beneath me, and he lifts my hips, bracing himself up on his elbows as he grips my ass in his giant hands. When he squeezes my cheeks, it spreads them apart, and I suck in a breath as he places the flat of his tongue *there*, but I only have a split second to be embarrassed before the soothing balm of it overshadows everything else.

His movements aren't hurried, no matter how long this goes on, his tongue making long, languid trips from the very bottom of me to the hood of my clit. And just as my hips make their very first instinctive roll against his face, he lowers me back to the bed and crawls back up my body.

I look up at him from the puddle of goo I've become, feeling my drugged expression lift into a lazy smile.

"Feel better?" he murmurs, pressing a soft kiss to my lips then nuzzling his nose lightly against mine.

"Yeah," I breathe with a slow blink at how gorgeous he is above me.

He grins devilishly but then his face relaxes into a soft smile. "I'd give anything to make love to you right now, little mouse, but I want you to know I'll never hurt you. And in order to keep to that promise, your sweet little pussy needs to rest."

My heart thuds behind my ribs at the sincerity of his tone. "O-Okay," I whisper.

Suddenly, I'm on top of him, and I squeak at the swift way he's moved me into a straddle above his abs, and although I feel his massive erection against my ass cheek, it's when he pushes me down with his grip on my hips and my pussy lays flush with his stomach that I moan in comforting pleasure.

"I don't know if you have a heating pad or not, but after swim team practice, there's nothing better than alternating hot and cold on sore muscles," he explains as my eyes shut to focus on the hotness of his body heat soaking into my core.

I lower myself until my face is resting in the crook of his neck, and I breathe him in. "I don't know how I feel about anything cold on my ladybits, but the hot is definitely doing wonders," I murmur, hearing him chuckle, and then I literally start to purr as his big hands begin to move up and down my naked back, rubbing and gently kneading me until I have to sip my drool back from the corner of my mouth before it drips on him. He laughs again but keeps up with what he's doing.

"Is this what it's always like between a Dom and his sub?" he asks quietly, and I try to shrug, but I only have the energy to twitch my shoulder.

"Not always. And I wouldn't know outside the club. I've never had anyone in my bed before," I confess.

"So you've never been in an actual relationship with a Dominant before?" His fingers trail along my spine, making me shiver.

"No. I've never even had sex with a Dom besides at the club."

He hums deep inside his chest as if considering my words. "Was that by choice? Like you consciously made the decision you would keep that part of yourself outside your home?" he asks, and it's almost like he sounds a bit guilty.

I pull my face out of his neck so I can look into his eyes, my head still resting on his shoulder, and he tilts his head so he can see me. "Why do you ask?" I prompt, wanting to know what he's thinking.

"Did I force you to fuck up your... I don't know, like... your safe place?" he asks, and I know the guilt I heard previously wasn't a figment of my imagination.

"You didn't force me to do anything, Nate," I reply, wanting him to know there's a big difference between domination and non-consent. "I didn't have to let you into my home last night. We could've had our conversation outside the club on the street. We could've gone to an all-night diner. Hell, we could've had it anywhere. I made the conscious decision to let you follow me home."

"That doesn't negate the fact that I might've fucked you in the one place you never wanted to fuck," he says, and I flinch, his words feeling like a stab to my heart, since before he called what we shared making love. He sees the hurt, and his arms come around me when I try to move off him, one hand burying in the back of my hair when I try to look away, forcing me to look into his eyes instead. "That came out harsher than I intended, and I apologize, Evelyn," he says low, and I blink away the stupid tears in my eyes. "What I meant was, I'm feeling somewhat guilty over the fact that I might've... sullied your sanctuary, and I hope it doesn't make your own home feel less... safe."

I swallow, and after a beat I nod as much as his hand in my hair will allow. "I... I had told myself that I would never bring just random guys back to my place. All D/s scenes would always take place at the club, and if somehow I started a relationship, only then would I consider letting them come home with me. So far, after two years of being a member, there's never been anything more than scenes. It's not exactly a breeding ground for developing serious feelings when all the members want to keep their identities close to the vest. Hence the masks and nicknames."

His brow furrows. "The girl at the club called you Eve," he points out.

"Close enough to my real name when I first started going that I would still recognize and answer to it if someone were speaking to me, but I figured people would just assume the nickname came from Eve, as in Adam's wife," I explain.

"Clever." He keeps ahold of the back of my head but loosens his grip around me to pick up with my backrub.

His features still look a little troubled, and for some reason, I want to soothe him, even though this is all happening because he's blackmailing me.

That's a lie and you know it.

I push the thought away, because I *don't* know that. He still has information that could destroy my life, and he's said nothing about keeping it a secret.

"I... I've always dreamed about what it would be like to have an actual relationship with a person like me. Well, not like *me*, but my other half. A real D/s relationship, not just sex. Every day, not just at the club," I tell him, and he meets my eyes again.

"How so? If it's not sex, what else is there when it comes to Doms and subs?" he asks, looking intrigued.

I lick my lips, and his eyes follow the movement. "I'm not just a submissive in bed, Nathaniel. It's... it's who I am as a person. It's the very core of me. To be in a D/s committed relationship would be... a dream. But I've never met anyone who made me feel anything... inside. I mean, yes, physical pleasure. But I never connected with someone who I felt could be my other half outside of sex." I refrain from telling him that I felt all those feelings and more last night and this morning, when he seemed to be able to read my mind, to know what I wanted and needed before I even thought about it.

"I know what you mean." His brow furrows as he stares off, not seeming to see the room around us. "It's like that emptiness I felt even right after having sex, like there was a huge part missing and the physical part did nothing to make up for it." And then his eyes meet mine. "Until I finally got to have you," he murmurs, saying exactly what I'd kept hidden.

I bite my lip, unsure what to say. It all seems way too fast and under terrible circumstances to tell him what I'm really feeling. He could hurt me in so many ways, not just my career and reputation, not just the potential loss of my membership, but he could break my heart. And I don't know if I could come back from that after how long and how much work it took to regain some semblance of myself after losing the only other people in my life I ever loved.

"It can't just be me feeling this way, Evie," he says low. "There's nothing you could say to convince me that last night was just like any other night you have at that club." His nostrils flare, and his hand tightens a little more on my hair.

I can't lie to him. No matter how badly I want to protect myself and all this man could destroy, I cannot look him in the eye when he's made himself this vulnerable and lie to his face about what I'm feeling.

"It's not just you, Nate," I whisper, and for some reason, tears spring to my eyes. My chin wobbles, and his image gets blurry. "It's not. And that scares the hell out of me, because you could ruin me. You could ruin my life after I've worked so hard to become happy again after I lost everything." A sob leaves me, and I squeeze my eyes shut and try to turn my face into his neck to hide.

CHAPTER 13

Nate

Her confession is like a defibrillator to my heart, shocking me to life. I flip us easily, and I stare down into her eyes swimming with tears, her little nose turning red along with her cheeks. She tries to look away, but I hold her tight, not allowing her to hide.

"I'm an idiot. I'm just a stupid guy who's never had to care about anyone else's feelings but my own. I get anything I want because of who I am, and even when someone doesn't want to give me something I want, I always find a way to get it out of them," I tell her, the words coming out in a rush, and she sniffles.

"But I am my parents' child, and they are good people. I swear I'm not all bad." I shift between her thighs, trying to calm the erection that sprang to life just from being pressed against her. "I know everything I've done to you, said to you, teased you about all year has taught you nothing but the contrary, but I swear on my life I'd never do anything to hurt you, Evie. And I'd hurt anyone else who even thought to try," I growl, and her eyes widen.

"Nath—"

"No. I'm serious. Think about it. All those lazy fucks at school who come into your library and leave it looking like shit—it's *me* who fixes their mess, just so you don't have to," I tell her.

She blinks. "I thought it was just part of your—"

"My OCD? No. My OCD only dictates *my* tidiness, *my* own messes, *my* own order. Have you ever seen me straightening Trenton's pencils and books when he's sitting beside me in study hall?"

"Well, no, but—"

"And have you ever seen me tucking in people's shirts or fixing their ties?"

"Also no—"

"That's because that shit doesn't bother me. What bothers me is them coming in there and forcing *my woman* to take care of them, when she should be focusing on pleasing *me*!" I growl ferociously, unable to keep my emotions in check, my breaths now sawing in and out of my lungs as the rage I feel causes the edges of my vision to vignette.

I don't know how long I stay like that, the anger radiating throughout my entire body. I can't get the unwanted, intrusive thoughts out of my head that my OCD causes to play on repeat, as I imagine people hurting Evelyn—physically causing her pain, fucking with her emotions, bringing her unnecessary stress. I'm stuck in the cycle, the uncontrollable thoughts repeating, repeating, over and over, making me angrier every time the reel starts over, making me want to screa—

"Your woman?" I hear Evie's voice in the distance. "This whole time, you've thought of me as your woman?"

The moment her palm cups my jaw, the repetitive thoughts stop on a dime, not even fading into the background; they're just... gone, and all I see is her.

"Nathaniel," she whispers. "Are you with me?" No fear, no cowering from the rage she couldn't have missed pouring off me, no horror in her eyes from seeing me get stuck in my intrusive thought cycle. She brings me back, and all I can do is nod.

She gives me a gentle smile, using her thumb to trace over my bottom lip, a gesture so sweet I don't even know how to process it. I've never let anyone touch me so tenderly before.

"So... no blackmail then?" She bites her lip.

I shake my head slowly. "No blackmail. You're secret is safe... even if you don't want me." I swallow.

Her chin wobbles even as she smiles, and she gives me a little nod. "Thank you, Nate."

"You're welcome, Evie."

We stay like that, just staring into each other's eyes, until she starts to squirm. "Am I too heavy?" I ask her, starting to lift my weight, but she tightens her grip on me, catching my bicep in her other hand to keep me close.

"No, it's not that," she says low, and then she turns shy, her cheeks turning pink.

"What is it, little mouse?" I ask, lowering so I can kiss her bottom lip that's red from her biting it.

"I... I um. Well...." She makes a nervous sound that's not quite a laugh.

"What is it, Evelyn?" I ask, making my tone more of a command, so maybe she'll have an easier time answering.

She swallows and meets my eyes shyly. "I want you. And I know I'm your sub and I shouldn't make any type of demand of you, and I should be satisfied after the amazing things we did last night, and usually I can only handle one night of scenes a week, but I just really feel... super close to you right now, and what I want more than anything in this world right now is for you to make love to me and—"

I slam my mouth down on hers, cutting off her nervous rambling, and kiss her with everything in me. I pour all the feelings I have for her into this kiss, and soon I'm aware of the way her hips are rocking beneath me.

I press my forehead to hers, our breaths quick and loud between us. "You saying you're mine, little mouse?" I ask, needing to confirm what I took from all those words she spewed.

She nods fast and shallow. "Yes, Mr. Black. I'm yours."

I shudder at her response, not believing this is actually happening, that my fantasy lover wants to be mine outside my dreams and not just for one night.

"But I don't want to hurt you, baby. You're so sore," I whisper, reaching down between us and cupping her pussy, finding her wet but still swollen.

"I don't care." She swallows. "I need you. Just... can you be gentle with me? I know you've always had to in the past, and I swear you can take me any other way you wish, but just this time—"

"Evie, I told you I'd never hurt you. And if you need soft and slow, if that's what my sub needs, then it's my job as your Dom to give you that, right?" I prompt, knowing I'd give her sweet and gentle even if it weren't part of being in this type of relationship.

She smiles, lifting her chin a little to nuzzle her nose against mine. "Right."

"Then that's what you'll get, little mouse. But that's going to be the first official rule between us, or law, or contract, or whatever the hell you call it," I add.

"And what's that?" She arches her back as I align my tip with her entrance.

"I don't give a fuck what other Doms have wanted in the past. You fucking tell me every time you want me," I order, and she gasps as I slowly start to sink inside her tight, wet heat.

"Yes, Sir," she hisses.

And I spend the next hour making sweet, slow, gentle love to my girl.

CHAPTER 14

Evie

"What do you want for lunch?" I hear Nate call from my library as I put away the few dishes I had in my dishwasher.

"Uuummm... maybe a salad from Salata? Or... oh, a pizza from Mod sounds yummy. Or I could fix us some sandwiches here. But all I have is turkey, so if you want something else.... We could do Subway... or Jersey Mike's—"

"Baby," he cuts me off, his voice so close it makes me jump, and I spin around from the cabinet to find his chest right behind me. I tilt my head back... back... back... until I finally meet his amused eyes.

I swallow. "Whatever you want is good," I whisper.

He narrows his eyes on me, looking for something he must find, because he nods once before leaning down to kiss my cheek. "I'll be right back with your lunch, milady," he says teasingly, and he disappears into my bedroom for a moment and comes back out tossing his keys up in the air and catching them as he makes his way to the door. When he opens it and steps outside, I expect to hear it close behind him, but instead, he peeks his head back in. "And don't. Get. Dressed," he orders with a lift of his eyebrow and an exaggerated look at my naked breasts before he pulls the door closed.

I giggle, shaking my head, and lean back against the counter, glancing down at myself. He'd at least allowed me to put panties on when he noticed how awkward I felt, feeling the wetness coating the inside of my thighs. It had made him instantly hard, seeing his cum dripping out of me, the insatiable man. But as much as I wanted him over and over, my ladybits had put their foot down. She was officially out of commission, no matter how gentle he could be. Gentle or not, the man was freaking huge, and my body was not used to getting so much undivided attention.

After he made love to me—in which I stayed completely coherent, thank goodness—we'd taken a shower together, where he did everything from washing my hair to exfoliating my back. We snuggled up on the couch, and after seeing my panic when he asked me what we should watch, he'd chosen something from my Watch Next list, a midseason episode of *Down to Earth with Zac Efron*. He commented on how everything on my list was reality or a documentary and told me those were his favorite programs too, and somehow it made me feel even closer to him.

That led to a discussion about other things we loved, finding we have all sorts of things in common, from different bands and music to books and hobbies. I found it incredibly sexy that he loves to read, which isn't a surprise, seeing as I'm a librarian. But when I thought back, I know he wasn't just telling me that, because he always has a book to read in study hall, and not just a textbook. There've been several times I've seen him leaned back in his chair with a worn-out paperback, the cover opened and folded around the back. At the time, I looked away, cringing at the book abuse, but that had been at a time when I didn't think there was much good in Nate Black. While it would still make my eye twitch to find him folding covers, at least now I'd find it forgivable, and I'd have the guts to tell him that isn't proper bibliophile etiquette.

I learned he was accepted into every college he applied to, including two Ivy League schools, but his dream and the one he's choosing to attend is the one not far from here, the university three generations of the Black family have attended.

"I want to stay close to home. I don't think my mom would handle it well if I moved too far away for college. I'm her only child," he said with a grin that softened into a smile when he looked at me. "And that means I won't be far from you either."

I sigh dreamily, pushing off the counter and going into my library to plop into my overstuffed chair. I pick up the book on my side table and pull out the bookmark, but replace it and put it back down when I realize I'm not retaining any of the words, because I can't stop thinking of Nathaniel.

Is it crazy to be this infatuated with someone who just yesterday I couldn't wait to spend the weekend away from? No doubt.

Is it possible that all those overwhelming feelings I ever had when it came to Nate was actually arousal I was fighting, because I thought it was wrong to feel it? Maybe.

And what kind of person does it make me that I'd be aroused by someone who tried to taunt and intimidate me every day? Normal, I guess, especially in Nathaniel's case. Aren't little girls always taught that when a boy picks on them, it means they like them? I always thought that was asinine to teach girls to accept a boy's bullying; if he likes you, he should show you respect and that he cares about you, not be mean. But haven't I always said that what Nate did to me wasn't quite bullying? And come to find out, he respects the hell out of me, and that's why he always cleans up after everyone in the library, not because of his OCD like I thought.

So it may seem like this is happening super-fast, but in reality, we've been playing this cat-and-mouse game for months. Months of—albeit fucked-up—flirting. Months of me coming home and thinking about him constantly. He made sure of that with his daily parting words. And it hadn't even been all bad thoughts either. I admired Nathaniel. He was so smart, so athletic, so undeniably attractive. I couldn't help but look up to him, and not because of his towering height. There was no denying he was going to be someone important one day, someone people respected, and I just couldn't for the life of me figure out why he wasted so much time picking on *me*. Every. Single. Day.

Now I know.

He wanted me. He had feelings for me he didn't understand, had never felt before. And combine that with having these Dominant urges deep inside him that he didn't know how to express, not to mention his OCD thrown in to muddy things up, he just had way too much going on and no idea what to do with everything.

While I'm relieved that everything is now out in the open, and after witnessing firsthand how my presence calms him, a soothing balm like Club Alias has always been for me, I can't help but wonder if it'd be smart to talk to someone about… all this. He's so young, just eighteen, even though he's ridiculously mature for his age. I can't help but worry that he may be too young to truly understand what it's like to be in an adult relationship. Especially one in which he'd be responsible in a way a Dominant needs to be for his sub.

I decide that when he gets back, I'll ask him how he'd feel about going to talk to Dr. Walker. If he's willing to go to my therapist and let Doc get a read on him—someone who isn't blinded by the emotions I'm feeling for Nate—then that would show me he's at least willing to take this seriously. If he fights me on it or simply refuses, then I'll know to protect myself and try to think of this as a physical relationship only.

Twenty minutes later, I'm starting to worry that Nate isn't coming back, that all of this was just some fucked-up game he's played to taunt and fuck with my mind like he's been doing all year. It shouldn't be taking this long just to run and get some food really quick. I don't even have his phone number to send him a text to check on him.

And when those thoughts enter my mind, they start rolling around and escalating, snowballing and becoming worse and worse. My anxiety takes over, and soon I know I'll be having a full-on panic attack. I'm pacing throughout my house, adjusting books on the shelf in my library, washing the spoon rest on my stove that was already clean, folding the laundry Nathaniel told me not to worry about after he started a load earlier this afternoon—towels he used to dry us off last night along with everything else in my hamper.

Right when I'm about to go into my room and get dressed, sure he's not going to return and he's somewhere laughing, telling all his friends that I'm this dumbass walking around my house topless while I wait for him... I hear my front door open, and I spin around to see his smiling face, his arms loaded down with bags and bags of takeout.

When his eyes meet mine where I'm trembling in the hallway, his expression falls, and he drops everything on the kitchen counter as he strides past it and toward me. He pulls me against him, his arm wrapping around the small of my back so when he straightens it lifts me onto my toes. His long fingers slide up into my hair from my nape and he tilts my head back to look into my eyes, his brow furrowed.

I swallow, blinking back the tears that had started to form in my panic. "I... I didn't think you were coming back," I confess, seeing the question in his eyes.

And he doesn't laugh at me. He doesn't make light of my worry or tease me. He doesn't do any of that. He absorbs it, seems to catalogue my feelings and file it for future use, and he nods and lowers his face to kiss me gently on the lips. When he pulls back, I've stopped shaking, and his eyes are soft when he tells me, "I'll always come back, little mouse."

I take a stuttered breath in and huff it out in a nervous laugh. "Sorry I'm such a frea—"

"Stop," he barks, and my teeth clack shut my mouth closes so abruptly. "You're not a freak. I took way longer than I should have." He moves his hand in my hair to where he cups the side of my neck and pets my jawline with this thumb. His eyes soften once more, and one corner of his sexy lips lifts into a half smile. "Gonna need them digits, Ms. Richards, so I call you if I'm running late."

I'm so relieved and at the same time overwhelmed by the rollercoaster of emotions I've just been on that I snort then giggle. "Just as long as you put me in your contacts as something other than that."

He lifts a brow, letting go of my face, but keeps me tight to him with the arm around my back, and he reaches into his pocket. With a few swipes and touches, he asks, "Number?" and I give it to him. A couple taps later, he turns the phone around to face me with a smirk. In place of a name, there's the word **MINE** in all caps surrounded by two little mouse emojis. "Incognito enough?" he prompts.

"That'll do," I say through my smile.

He turns the phone back to him and works his thumb across the screen, and a second later, I hear my ringtone coming from my purse by the front door. "And now you have mine." He kisses me once more then gently lets me go, taking hold of my hand and tugging me over to the bags on the kitchen counter.

"What... in the world?" I murmur, my eyes going wide.

"Well, I picked up on the fact that you're not the best at multiple choice," he says with a wink, "so I thought, why choose? And I got us a little bit of everything." He gestures to all the bags like he's a game show model, and a smile spreads across my face. "I think after we get to know each other a little better, I won't even need to ask. I'll just feed you something I know you'll like. Sound good?"

And it's like my dream man has been dropped from the heavens and into my kitchen. I nod, choked up a little. "Sounds perfect. Thank you."

"Uuumm... your kitchen table's a little small, baby. Want to do this picnic style in the living room while we watch another episode?" When my mouth opens and closes like a fish a couple times, he chuckles. "Scratch that." He clears his throat and deepens his voice with a lifted brow, but there's a mischievous twinkle in his eyes. "We're going to eat this picnic style in the living room while we watch another episode. Please grab us some utensils, little mouse."

"Yes, Sir," I reply, and circle around the bar to the drawer that holds my set of forks and knives. "Are there napkins in the bags?"

"I'm pretty sure there's enough napkins in all these bags for you to have a lifetime supply. We'll never have to buy napkins ever again," he tells me, and I like the way it sounds as if he means we'll be living together at some point.

When I reach the living room, he's pulled my coffee table out into the center of the room and is setting out a buffet's worth of food. Two pizzas with different toppings, three sandwiches sliced in half, two salads with a selection of dressings, and four different flavors of cookies. He pulls out two bottles of water, showing me the label as I sit on the floor at one end of the coffee table.

"Spring water, not purified," he explains, when my brow furrows, and I grin.

"Someone took Zac Efron's lesson to heart," I reply, reminded of the episode we watched this morning about the different kinds of water, and how purified bottled water is actually really bad for you.

"Learning occurred," he confirms, and he lowers his towering frame until he's sitting cross-legged and facing the TV. "Dig in, beautiful."

My face heats at the compliment, and I reach for one of the salads, asking him to pass me the ranch dressing. We eat and watch the next episode, and I can't help but take in how natural this feels, eating and watching TV, topless no less, with Nate on a Saturday afternoon. As exciting and new as it is, it also seems like we've done this a million times.

"Let me try," he states and leans in my direction, opening his mouth while his hands are full of pizza. I get a bite on my fork with a little bit of everything in the salad and feed it to him, and I beam when he hums with pleasure. "Now that's a damn good salad."

I nod, smiling shyly as I look down into my plastic bowl.

"Here, try this."

I look up to see the pizza in front of my face, and my eyes meet his as I lean forward and take a bite. "Mmm," I moan and nod while I chew. After I swallow, I lick my lips. "That's really good. What toppings are on that?"

"Ground beef, red onions, and green bell peppers," he replies, watching my lips.

I smile again, saying softly, "Please put that on my list of food choices."

"Done, little mouse." He says it so nonchalantly that it settles all the anxiety that was still lingering after I thought he wasn't coming back.

When we're done, we work side by side to clean up the mess, even though I offered to do it while he relaxed. He just gave me a stern look that shut me up, and everything was back to the way it was before we ate in a matter of minutes.

I go sit down on the couch in the living room, and he disappears down my hallway, coming back a moment later with a scowl on his face. I sit up straight in alarm he looks so serious. "What's the matter?"

He crosses his arms over his chest and lowers his eyebrows, and I shrink back into the couch at the look, having no idea what would cause him to look at me that way.

"There's no laundry in the dryer," he states, and his tone makes me swallow.

"I-I... well, you were taking so long, and I clean when I get worrie—"

He cuts me off, "I told you I would fold everything once it was done. No matter the circumstances, I feel like... I feel like there should be some type of punishment for you disobeying me."

I bite my lip, taking in the emotions warring in his eyes. This is all new to him. This is a part of a Dominant's life I've never seen before, the path they've taken to become the trained and professional Doms I've only met at Club Alias. I don't know any of their backstories. I don't know what led to them being the flawless and perfect leaders they are now. It's like... it's like Nathaniel is a baby Dom, finding his way, finding his voice, finding his strength and getting used to this new skin.

I think of the book I love, the one by Red Phoenix, and how it followed the heroine in her training to become the perfect submissive. And at one point, they had to scene with the Doms in training, who were in a separate class. It reminds me that Doms don't just... materialize as perfect beings. They have to be taught just as I had to learn how to be a proper sub.

It makes me realize that if we truly want to make this work, he's going to need someone to teach him, and that someone can't be me.

I nod, sitting up straight and placing my hands in my lap. "Yes, Mr. Black," I finally say, and he reaches behind him and rubs the back of his neck.

"Um... so, uh... come here." He crosses his arms once more, and I stand and walk over to him, wondering what he'll do. He doesn't look like he even knows it himself. When I'm directly in front of him, he looks down at me, and we stand there looking into each other's eyes for long moments, the tension growing thick.

Finally, he shakes his head. "We really need to figure this out, little mouse," he murmurs.

I nod slowly, hiding the relief I feel that he's mature enough that he wants to take this seriously, that he doesn't just take this as some role-playing game to liven up his sex life. "I know someone," I tell him softly.

His eyebrows perk. "Who is it?"

"My therapist, Dr. Walker. He um..." I trail off, knowing I signed a non-disclosure agreement and am not supposed to say anything to anyone I wouldn't be willing to sponsor and vouch for.

"He what, little mouse?" he prompts, and when he sees I'm battling my next words to say, he closes the tiny space between us. "You can trust me, Evelyn. I swear on my life. I want to learn. I want to be good at this, to become the perfect Dom for you. To understand what I am inside."

I melt against him at the plea in his eyes, and I nod. "Dr. Walker is one of the owners of Club Alias. There's a process to become a member, but once you are, once you've been vetted, then there are classes, private lessons, and therapy sessions you can continue after his initial assessment that can teach you everything you need to know."

The relief on his face makes me whimper, and I can't stop myself from reaching up and pushing his dark hair out of his eyes before cupping his cheek. All the worry I had before about him refusing to talk to Doc disappears, and for the first time, I feel like this really might work between us.

He clears his throat and looks at me sternly once again. "Set me up the earliest appointment Dr. Walker has available. Um... any day after 3:30 p.m. works. Actually, any time works. I'll just get a doctor's note. The sooner the better," he says, and I pull my lips between my teeth to keep from giggling at the fact that my Dom is a high school senior.

Of all the men in the BDSM community, some of them the best in the entire world right here in my hometown, I had to have an undeniable connection with an untrained eighteen-year-old.

"I'll set that up now," I reply, but when I go to turn around and get my phone, he catches my wrist and halls me to him.

"Just know the only reason I'm not punishing you right now is because I feel like what you went through while I was gone was punishment enough. But once I learn more about being a proper

Dominant, you won't get away with such disobedience so easily," he promises, and I melt against him.

"Yes, Mr. Black," I breathe. And he leans down and kisses me soundly before spinning me around and swatting me on my ass, sending me in the direction of my purse.

It's all I can do not to giggle like a schoolgirl.

CHAPTER 15

Nate

Evie sent her therapist a text requesting an appointment as soon as possible, and once she told him it wasn't any type of emergency for her mental health, he set us up for Tuesday at 4:00 p.m. I'd have to miss swim practice, but I knew it would be worth it. This is something I need to do, not only to learn for myself but to prove to Evie how serious I am about all of it, about us.

I spent the night again that night, assuring her my parents wouldn't be worried, because I told them I was spending the weekend at Alistor's house. We didn't have sex again, because I'd worn the poor little thing out, but that didn't stop me from eating her until she came. I was good and thoroughly obsessed with Evelyn's pussy.

Seeing as I spent the last two days in the same clothes, on Sunday I got to enjoy watching Evie blush for two hours as I walked around buck-ass naked while my stuff was being washed and dried. I have no shame, and it was amusing seeing her squirm and try not to stare.

We had a long discussion about how things would go after our weekend together. I promised her I wouldn't tell anyone about us, reiterated the fact that I wouldn't tell anyone anything about her secret, and was sworn secrecy about Club Alias. If the place was so important to Evie, then I would make it important to me, so she had nothing to worry about there.

She wondered aloud what it would be like during study hall, now that I know what she looks like naked. I told her that wasn't so much to worry about, more being the fact that we'd had butt sex. She'd choked on her sip of coffee. But on a more serious note, I told her if we truly wanted to keep us under wraps then I'd have to continue treating her the way I always had in front of everyone. Yet I made it perfectly clear that it would all be an act so not to let her anxiety talk her into it being anything besides that.

In reality though, I have no idea how that will go. Taunting her, intimidating her now that I know the most vulnerable parts of her, that she knows the deepest and darkest parts of me... it just doesn't feel right. So we'd just have to take all that one day at a time.

Now, it's Monday morning. Six hours until study hall and T-minus thirty-two hours until our appointment with Dr. Walker. Every time I glance at my watch, I have to do the math quickly for both countdowns before I can focus back on my schoolwork.

It's driving me mad knowing Evelyn is just right down the hall in the library. After sleeping with her in my arms for two nights straight, I could barely fall asleep last night, my California king-sized bed feeling way too big when I'd been curled around my little mouse in her queen. When I got up this morning, I made sure to use the cologne she mentioned she likes. I would've put a little more effort into looking good for her, but seeing as we're a uniformed school and I already make sure I look my very best every day, all I could really do this morning is wear my new white polo shirt instead of one of my older ones.

When I came downstairs after getting ready for school, I skidded to a stop next to my mom and pulled her in for a hug, something I realized I hadn't done in a while when she looked at me with a surprised but happy smile on her face. I told her she looked pretty today and that she did an excellent job on dinner last night, practicing verbally praising so I could get used to doing it for Evie. Mom had flustered and swatted at me playfully, telling me to hurry before I was late for school—as if I had ever been late for anything in my life.

I spent hours on the internet last night looking up everything BDSM. There was a whole world of information, and it was easy to get overwhelmed trying to take in everything at once, so I chose one thing to focus on in a guide I found about becoming a worthy Dom, and I gave myself an assignment. Anytime something good stands out to me, I won't keep my thoughts on the inside. I will verbally give praise. Basically, a sub lives for praise, so I need to train myself to speak up when something makes me happy.

So far, I've complimented my mom, two teachers, told Mr. Garland the janitor that he was doing an excellent job on the floors, and Trevor that his hair looked good today, to which he called me gay, but whatever. Love is love.

Three hours until study hall. Twenty-nine until our appointment.

Two hours until study hall. Twenty-eight until our appointment.

An hour and thirty-two minutes until study hall. Twenty-seven hours and thirty-two minutes until our appointment.

And hour and fourteen minutes until study hall. Twenty-seven hours and fourteen minutes until our appointment.

And on and on it continues, the closer I get to study hall, the more frequently I'm checking my watch and doing the math, obsessing, compulsively counting down, and I pray it won't be like this every day from now until the end of the schoolyear, because I can barely concentrate in class when all I hear and see inside my mine is a clock ticking down the minutes.

Finally, the bell rings, and I jump up from my desk so quickly I almost knock the chair over. Books in bag, pencil behind ear, chair pushed in. I take off out of the classroom and down the hall to the library, arriving just in time for the door to burst open as the previous study hour class floods out. I can't get through them, feeling like I'm swimming upriver, so I stand back against the wall until they're all through, and then I shove through the door, my eyes immediately seeking her out.

There she is, inside the circular circulation desk, and I don't know if it always looked this way, if it's the lighting, or if I just see her a little differently, clearly now, but she looks like a fucking angel.

Evie's in her standard uniform of a primly button-up white blouse and slacks, but for the first time ever, her hair is pulled up out of her beautiful face in a curly bun on top of her head. She's wearing her glasses again for the first time since Friday at school, but the fact that her hair is up tells me she did it just for me, after I told her I loved it that way.

I don't know how long I stand there just staring at her, but soon the door opens up behind me, and Trevor playfully shoves my back, so I take a step forward and out of the way. "You coming creeper?" he asks when he gets a few steps in front of me, and I roll my eyes at him, following him over to our table. I set out my notebook, two pencils, and slide the third pencil from behind my ear, aligning it with the others, and then hang by backpack on my chair.

Before I slide out my chair and take a seat, I clear my throat. "Gonna go fuck with the nerd," I tell him like I always do, and he waves me off, paying me no mind. I stroll up to the desk without making a sound, so when she turns around, I'm standing so close to her, only the three feet of wood between us, that she genuinely startles and takes a step back, her hand going to her chest. The book in her other hand drops to the floor, and she looks down at it, her glasses slipping down her nose a little. I smirk when she looks back up at me with a little frown on her perfect lips, and I lean down on the desk when she bends to pick it up.

"Nice hair, Ms. Richards," I say, not bothering to keep my voice low, since I'd said the same thing to Trevor this morning, and she jerks her head up from her squatted position, her hand feeling around blindly for the book.

"Th-Thank you, Mr. Black." She swallows. "Nathaniel," she corrects, and my smirk grows into a wide smile, because it dawns on me she's always done that—and now I know it was always her submissive showing through.

"A little to the right," I tell her, and at her confused look, I point downward twice. "Your book."

"Huh? Oh." She finally looks back down and snatches up the book before standing abruptly. "Will you be needing help with anything, Nathaniel?" she asks quietly, pushing her glasses back up and looking around with just her eyes as if trying to see if we're being watched.

"I'll let you know... Ms. Richards." I grin, winking at her, and I see her relax oh-so-subtly before she nods and gets back to what she was doing.

I go back to my table, pull my chair out, and relax into my seat, feeling a peace come over me now that I'm in her presence. All the anxiousness I've felt all day counting down the hours then minutes until I got to see her again dissipates, and so I flip open my notebook and finish the work I wasn't able to concentrate on in my last two classes.

Halfway through the study hour, I look up to see Evie isn't behind the circulation desk, and I glance around to see where she's gone. Trevor is distracted, working on something with one of our classmates, and no one else is paying me any attention, so I stand and go in search of my little library mouse. I walk down the center aisle between bookcases, not seeing her anywhere on the first floor, so I take the wooden staircase to the second, measuring my steps so it looks like I'm just perusing the shelves. It's not out of character for me, seeing how I love to read, so if anyone were to look up through the balcony, they wouldn't think twice about it.

And then I spot her, at the very back of one of the rows, putting away a stack of books in her arms. I wait until she's done so I don't risk making her drop one, which would be loud and call attention to us, and then I start toward her. She looks up when I'm halfway down, and she stops in her tracks. I'm proud of her when she doesn't take a step back; just the small fidget of her pushing her glasses into place is the only sign of her nervousness.

"You look beautiful, little mouse," I murmur, turning to face the bookshelf and straightening a couple that were pushed slightly farther back than the others.

"Thank you," she replies in that sweet voice of hers, and I glance at her long enough to catch her shy smile.

"You wear your hair back for me, baby?" I pull a book off the shelf and turn it over as if I'm reading the blurb on the back.

I see her shift on her feet in my peripheral vision, and hear her whisper, "Just for you."

I close my eyes, trying to fight off the instant arousal, and when I'm unsuccessful, I reach down and adjust my semihard cock. She whimpers.

There are so many things I want to say to her, so many things I want to tell her I learned last night while I was studying the lifestyle, but when I open my mouth, I'm interrupted.

"There you are!"

We both look down the aisle to see Mr. Newman, one of the English teachers, coming toward us.

"Oh shit," she whispers, and I almost laugh at her sweet voice cursing only loud enough for me to hear before she steps away from me and says louder, "Mr. Newman, what can I help you with?"

"Oh, not you, my dear. I've been looking for Mr. Black here," he explains, taking out a handkerchief and wiping his sweaty forehead.

I turn to face him, keeping my internal grimace off my face when I see him stuff the material back into his pocket. God only knows the last time he washed that thing. The portly man is a wonderful teacher, but goddamn, handkerchiefs are disgusting and unsanitary. I keep the book in my hands so he doesn't try to shake one.

"Mr. Newman?" I prompt.

"Nathaniel, your report you turned in last week was astounding, and so I turned it in for a scholarship contest. You've been chosen as a finalist, and I just wanted to let you know they'll be selecting the winner next week!" he tells me, and I give him an obligatory smile, even though I'd rather him just go away so I can have this private moment with my woman.

"That's amazing news," Evie says, picking up on exactly what I'm thinking and filling in the words for me so I don't have to lie and act happy that he interrupted us.

Mr. Newman nods. "You're going to do great things, Mr. Black."

And I hear Evie giggle for a split second before she covers it with a super fake-sounding sneeze.

A LESSON IN BLACKMAIL

"Oh, bless you, dear. The second floor can get pretty dusty. Next time I run detention, I'll send the little buggers your way, and you can put them on cleaning duty," he tells her.

"Thank you, sir," she says, and I look at her with a raised eyebrow, jealousy making my nostrils flare. She glances up and sees it, and she jerks her head Mr. Newman's way, opening and closing her mouth like a fish. "Uhh... is there anything else?" she asks him.

"Nope, that's it. Guess I got my cardio for the day!" He chuckles and lifts his arm high in order to pat me on the shoulder. And I barely refrain from wiping off where his sweaty palm had touched me.

"Thank you, Mr. Newman. See you tomorrow," I tell him, and he waves over his shoulder as he's already heading back down the aisle. When we hear him make his way down the stairs, I put the book back on the shelf where it goes then turn to face Evie.

I don't even have to say anything before she's fidgeting. "My parents raised me to be polite. You can't go getting all... puffed up and growly every time I call a male elder 'sir.'" She's so flustered it's adorable.

"Puffed up and... growly, Ms. Richards?" I smirk.

"Well... maybe not. But you would've been if we hadn't been at school." She punctuates the end with one nod, and I have to fight not to laugh at her haughtiness.

"God, you're so fucking cute when you try to be mad at me," I tell her, and she pushes up her glasses once again and then balls her little fists at her sides.

She whispers, "We're really going to have to figure this out." She shifts on her feet. "You seem to like when I speak my mind, but other times...." She doesn't finish that sentence. "It's very confusing. I don't know what I'll be punished for or when, and it's... it's not good for my...." She pulls out the buttoned collar of her blouse, her face flushing.

Seeing she's really rattled, I close the distance between us, uncaring if anyone were to see us if my woman is really starting to panic. She comes first. Always. Everyone else be damned, even myself.

"Baby," I murmur, cupping her jaw, and she relaxes fractionally. "How about, for now, we keep the punishments and such for the week-

115

ends? Once we really get a grip on this thing between us, we'll hash it all out and make up our own rules. I'm sure that's something Doc will be able to help us with, right?"

She nods, relaxing further. "Right."

"Very good," I tell her. And I glance around and behind me before sneaking in a quick kiss then letting her go.

Back in my seat, I spend the rest of the hour following Evie around with my eyes, like I've always done. Only instead of doing it to fuck with her, now it's to admire the graceful line of her body as she works. It's to watch for the smiles she gives few and far between, when she gave them to me readily all weekend. It's to give her a little smirk when she glances my way, letting her know I caught her looking. It's to watch her expression change when she gazes off into space, and I know she's thinking of my cock inside her from the way her face flushes crimson.

When the bell rings and everyone files out, I no longer slam in their left-out chairs with a murderous look in their direction. I push each one in and keep my eyes on Evie while she watches me with a dreamy look on her perfect face.

When I'm done, I walk up to her desk and bend over it like I always do. And I know my parting words should be just as taunting as they always are, because that's just who I am, and I'll always love to watch her squirm.

"So, Ms. Richards," I start, and she licks her plump lips.

"Yes, Nathaniel?" she prompts, and I lift my brow at her unhesitant use of my first name.

"Have you checked your texts today?" I ask, knowing the teachers keep their cells locked away in drawers of each of their desks per school policy.

"I have not," she replies, shifting in her cute little leather flats, so different from the sky-high sexy stilettos she was wearing Friday night, and I find I love both versions of my woman just the same.

"You should do that soon," I tell her, standing up from her desk and glancing around to make sure no one else is around to hear us. "Oh, and Ms. Richards?"

"Yes, Nathaniel?"

I give her my mischievous grin, looking at her from beneath my brow. "How's that sweet little pussy today?"

I spin on my heel and walk to the door, laughing loudly at the look of shock on my little mouse's face.

CHAPTER 16

Evie

"Don't be a dick pic. Don't be a dick pic. Don't be a dick pic," I chant as I unlock the bottom drawer of my desk and pull it open to reach in my purse and grab my phone. No one has come into the library yet, so I sit down in my rolling chair and hold up my phone, ignoring all the notifications on my lock screen and closing my eyes after the facial recognition unlocks it.

I breathe out a cleansing breath and open them, touching the Messages app.

There's only one, and it's an image from Nate.

"Don't be a dick pic. Don't be a dick pic..." I whisper, and then I tap on the message.

And nearly drop my phone.

It's not a dick pic. Of course it's not. Nathaniel may be an eighteen-year-old male with a seemingly insatiable sexual appetite, but he's also a classy and respectable man. I should've known he wouldn't send me a dick pic. But what he did send me makes me wipe the drool from the corner of my lips.

The picture is of him lying in bed, shirtless, his white sheets pushed oh-so-low on his hips. He took it from his perspective, so I can see everything from the wide, smooth planes of his chest, over the ripple of his abdomen, past the V of those godlike muscles, and I can just make out the outline of his thick, long cock beneath the covers.

I close my eyes and blow air out through pursed lips, pulling the phone to my chest. Never in my life have I been with such a perfect specimen of masculinity. Never in my life has *any* man wanted me or treated me the way Nate does, much less one who looks like *this*. Is this fate rewarding me for dealing me such a shitty hand before?

The loud bang of the library door being pushed open startles me from my daydreaming, and I quickly toss my phone back in the drawer and lock it, standing from my seat and welcoming the last class of the day. Being Monday, I'll still have to stay another hour and a half after school ends for those students who need the library to do their work, and I can't help but wonder what Nathaniel will be doing once the day ends.

Two and a half hours later, I'm locking the library door behind me, and I make my way down the long hallway, the red and black lockers on either side of me making me pause once I reach the ones near the restroom. In the very center of them is the silhouette of a cougar, the school's mascot, and I stop and stare. Pulling my leather planner up to my chest, I hug it as I realize something, and I start to giggle. Standing here and laughing like an idiot, I'm sure I'd look insane to anyone who came upon me, but I can't help it.

Being twenty-two with an eighteen-year-old lover... does that make me a cougar?

I stop laughing and really think about it. I don't know for sure. Is any woman with a younger man called a cougar? Or is there a certain number of years that has to span between them for it to count? There are only four between Nate and me, really just a blip of time if you think about it. It won't seem like a big deal when I'm like... twenty-nine and he's twenty-five. Even less when I'm thirty-seven and he's thirty-three. Whatever the case, I find it hysterical that our school mascot just happens to be a cougar.

I continue on my way down the hall, passing classrooms and then the gym, turning a corner to head toward the door closest to the staff parking lot, and I hear a whistle blow, muffled behind glass doors that are fogged over. The door to the indoor swimming pool where the swim team practices. I don't know Nate's practice schedule, but knowing he's the star of the team, I can't help but wonder if he's in there. Before I even realize what I'm doing, I push the door open and step inside, the humidity of the huge room making me take in a thick breath that smells like chlorine, instantly feeling clammy.

I step farther in, seeing four or five bodies sail through the water, nothing but their black swim caps and goggles visible besides their powerful arms pulling them to the opposite side of the pool. Coach Gauntt sits on a diving board, her whistle between her lips and a stopwatch in her hand. When the swimmers reach the end nearest her, she blows the whistle in a short, loud burst and then reads off the time, and I see two of the athletes high-five before they all pull themselves out of the water using the cement edge.

I recognize Nate's body instantly, even though his sexy hair is covered in the black swim cap and his eyes are covered in goggles. He's several inches taller than everyone else, and I feel my face heat when my eyes lower to his black Speedo, my heart doing a little flip knowing exactly what he's packing inside the black material. Even from an Olympic-size pool of distance, his body makes mine tingle, especially now that I've felt what it can do to me. He's like a magnet, and my feet move me closer to him without my telling them to do so. I'm more than halfway to him when I'm stopped in my tracks.

"Evie?" I hear a female voice call my name, and my eyes pull up to Coach Gauntt's position on the diving board. "You need something, hun?"

My mouth parts, and all that comes out is a stupid-sounding "Uhhh…" as my eyes go back to Nate, who has turned my way, and he lifts his goggles from his eyes, letting them sit on top of his cap. His lips twisting in a little smirk makes my pussy clench.

"You okay, Evie?" Coach Gauntt prompts again, and the last thing I want is for one of my coworkers to think I'm some kind of idiot, so I spit out the first thing that pops into my head.

"Um… yeah. I was just wondering if the pool has open swim hours.

I uh… my gym doesn't have an indoor one, and it's gotten too cold to use the outdoor one." That sounded believable, right? I mean, I don't even go to a gym, but surely that would be a thing. At least I hope so.

"Oh, yeah, sweetie. Right there on the wall." She points to the other side of the pool to where there's a bulletin board covered in papers.

I nod and head back the way I'd come, turning the corner at the end of the pool and squeezing my planner tighter to my chest when I feel his eyes following me.

The sound of Coach Gauntt's whistle makes me jump, and I hurry faster to the board when I hear her yell, "Next up, boys!"

"Hey, Ms. Richards," one of my sweeter students greets me as I pass by where they're lining up to start their race.

"Good luck, Alex," I reply quietly, and make my way closer to the bulletin board. When I finally reach it, I let out the breath I'd been holding and force myself to focus and look for the pool hours, even though I have absolutely no intention of ever coming here to swim.

Two things happen at once that nearly make me jump out of my skin.

Coach Gauntt blows her whistle loud and drawn out, and at the same time a long, muscled arm reaches over my shoulder, a hot and tall wet body stepping up behind me as Nathaniel points to a small rectangular sign on the corkboard, and I squeak, jerking around to face him. He towers over me, especially when I'm in my flats, and with every single one of his muscles on display, and with that darkly hungry look in his heart stoppingly gorgeous eyes, I step back into the wall, squeezing my leather planner to my chest like my life depends on it.

He lowers his voice, looking me in the eyes. "This looks very precarious, little mouse." I swallow at his words. "Turn back around and act like what I'm saying is interesting as fuck."

My inner muscles squeeze, enough to show me I'm not nearly as sore I was yesterday. I do as he says without pause, feeling the water droplets from his chest sink into my shirt at the top of my shoulders, and I shudder.

"Did you come looking for me, Ms. Richards?" he asks me, and I answer truthfully.

"I was heading to my car, and then suddenly I was here, like I was drawn to you."

I see his bicep flex, hear him blow out a breath above and behind me, and I feel it on my neck, giving me goose bumps. "Mmm, you don't know how good that makes me feel, sweet Evie," he whispers.

I reach down to rustle in my purse blindly, pulling my phone out. When I unlock it, the first thing that pops up is his picture, since I never closed out the Messages app. He sees it and chuckles as I scramble to close it out and open my Camera app, making a show of taking a picture of the hours sign.

I turn around, more controlled this time, and he smiles wickedly as he puts just enough space between us to not look suspicious. I glance toward Coach Gauntt out the corner of my eye, but she's not paying a bit of attention to anything other than her swimmers.

"I appreciate the photo you sent me, Mr. Black. It'll be very useful later," I say quietly, suddenly feeling ballsy and wanting to give him a dose of his own medicine at what my words might mean.

When I meet his eyes, they're blazing, his nostrils slightly flared. I swallow thickly, forcing myself to keep my posture, because he looks like he wants to eat me alive.

"You lay one finger on that pussy and there will be hell to pay... *Ms. Richards*," he growls low, and my eyes dart around to make sure no one is near us before I whisper my reply.

"Well then it's a good thing I have a vibrator, *Nathaniel*."

All of his muscles tense, and he starts to take a step toward me, but the loud shrill of the whistle being blown saves us both from whatever scene he was about to make.

"Next set!" Coach Gauntt yells, and Nate curses under his breath before stepping back.

He looks deep into my eyes, a warning on his face and in his tone. "I'll call you this evening."

I drop my phone into my purse and then pull it higher up on my shoulder, giving him a nod. "Good luck, Nate." I give him a little smile, my eyes twinkling when he narrows his eyes, leaving him wondering if I'm talking about the phone call or his race as I leave to head out to my car.

CHAPTER 17

Nate

Nothing could be better than Evelyn's complete surrender as I sink my cock deep into her scorching, wet, gripping pussy. Nothing. But after last night, I learned that playing power games with her when we're unable to be together is a close fucking second.

In my research, I learned the benefits of making a submissive hold out, setting a rule that they aren't allowed to give themselves pleasure without their Dom's explicit permission. The site I found romanticized it, making it sound delicious and intoxicating instead of clinical like a few of the other things I was reading sounded. And I'm man enough to admit I like the more fantastical version of the lifestyle better. Maybe it's the reader in me.

The article on the site said to think about it as if you own your submissive's pleasure. Their orgasms belong to their Dom. So if they were to have those orgasms without their Dom, it's like they're stealing them from him... or her... although a female version is called a Domme, or Dominatrix, or Fem Dom.... Actually, every site I came across called them something different, so I'm not sure. Not that it matters, since I never plan to be with one; I just like to absorb all the information I can find on a subject I'm interested in.

So after I called her last night, I made it clear that she wasn't allowed to come without me, but I promised her a reward if she was a good little sub and followed my rules. Since I'd be in her small town for our appointment with Dr. Walker this evening, there was nothing keeping me from making a pit stop at her house on my way back home afterward.

The day went about the same as yesterday—me compulsively counting down the time until study hall and our appointment, Evelyn's presence quieting the obsessive thoughts enough that I could finish my work once I got to the library. A stolen kiss between bookcases. Parting words that made her flush with desire. There was a sign on the circulation desk today letting students know that the head librarian would be absent today during the last class and afterhours but a substitute would be available, and reading it made my adrenaline surge in my veins knowing it was because she was leaving early to make it to our appointment at four.

I signed myself out in the main office at 2:45 p.m., and as I was walking to my truck in the student parking lot, I looked up when I heard a vehicle start in the next lot over, stopping to watch when I saw Evie back her little car out of the parking space. She must not have seen me, because she didn't stop to wave or anything on her way toward the exit, and then her car disappeared onto the main road. I picked up my pace, tossing my backpack into the passenger seat on my way in through the driver side, cranking my truck and connecting my phone to Bluetooth. I turned on Submersed, still stuck on the same album I've been listening to all week, since every time I hear the opening notes of "Hollow," I'm immediately filled with the memories of what took place the night I drove to Evelyn's house an hour away.

Which leads to this moment, and I'm trying my damnedest not to speed when I know my destination is far enough away from everyone we know that I'll be able to touch and kiss Evie without worrying we'll be caught. I'm a little nervous about the appointment. I've always been a little wary of therapists, knowing I'll have to spill my guts only for them to try to give me advice and pills to try to control my disorder. But this time, the feeling is different. There's a... hope inside me that's never been there before, something telling me that this really could be the key to helping me understand what and who I am inside.

Fifty-two minutes later, I pull into the parking lot behind Evie and park next to her, hopping out of the truck and beeping it locked before hurrying to her door to open it for her. Unlike last time, I don't have to coerce her out. I just hold out my hand, and she places her delicate little fingers in my palm. I haul her out of her seat and into my arms, my mouth landing on hers before she's even able to finish her squeak, and she melts against me as I dip my tongue inside her mouth.

She sighs when I finally pull back and let her slide down my body until her feet touch the ground. I glance at my watch, seeing we have a little more than fifteen minutes before our appointment. "Perfect timing," I tell her, and she gives me a small smile with understanding in her eyes. She must already have picked up on the fact that one of my quirks is always being early. "On time" registers as "late" in my mind. She bends to reach in and grab her purse, and I fight the urge to grab her ass, but only because I know it would probably lead to things that would cause us to be late. When she stands, I close the door for her and she locks her car, and I take her hand, loving the feel of how small it is in mine. I've never held hands with anyone but my parents when I was little, so the act feels new and intimate somehow.

When we enter the office, I instantly relax, the waiting room neat and orderly. It's not clinical like a lot of therapist offices. Even out here, there's a diffuser sending up steam that smells like eucalyptus, and the chairs look comfortable instead of stiff. Evie releases my hand to walk up to the woman behind the window who stood up when we entered and greets her with a smile.

"Good evening, Ms. Richards. How are you today?" the woman asks.

"I'm wonderful, Silvia," she tells her, and I take a seat in one of the chairs.

"You're all good for paperwork unless your insurance or address has changed. But if you'll have your partner fill out everything on this clipboard... and here's a pen," I hear Silvia say, and it makes me realize....

I lift my hand to my ear, and sure enough, there's no pencil. I'd been so excited to pack up and leave school that for the first time in... God, five? Six years? That I didn't have a pencil readily available, when normally one is there behind my ear until the moment I get undressed at home. Even on swim practice days, when I get dressed in the locker room afterward, the pencil is added almost like an accessory, and stays there until I'm hopping in my shower.

"You okay?" Evie asks softly, sitting beside me and handing me the clipboard and pen.

I turn my astounded look toward her and point to my ear. Her brow furrows, her eyes searching where I'm pointing, and then recognition masks her face and her expression goes soft when she smiles. She lifts her hand to my cheek, her thumb stroking my jaw.

"You good?" she prompts, and I know she's asking if I'm okay with the fact that I don't have my own pencil.

I nod, my eyes never leaving hers when I ask instead of answering, "What are you doing to me, little mouse?"

She giggles, seeing I'm not bothered in the slightest by the revelation, and leans in to place a sweet kiss on my lips before turning her attention to the clipboard in my hands. "Just fill all that out. It's the usual doctor junk. When we get inside with Doc, he'll have the NDA for you to sign," she tells me, and I turn my questioning eyes to her. "Everyone who wants to learn about you know where has to sign one, and if you decide you want to become a member, there will be a separate contract. But I won't get into all that. Let's just get through this first appointment and see what you think."

I nod once more and begin to fill out all the paperwork about my medical history and insurance. When I'm done, I take the clipboard up to the window with my insurance card and driver's license, and the woman makes a copy then hands them back to me, keeping the paperwork.

Soon, the door directly in front of the seats we're waiting in opens, and a beautiful blonde woman hurries out of the room, her face turning crimson when she looks up and sees us watching her. A tall man, maybe even taller than me but much wider, his shoulders seeming to fill the entire doorway, calls after the woman just as she reaches the front door.

"Be careful getting home, Astrid," he tells her, and she tucks her long, light hair behind her ear before giving him a nod then shoving her way through the door.

His hand shoots through his hair as he blows out a breath, and then his eyes turn to us. I'm surprised when Evie speaks up beside me. "Was that...?"

"Yep," he replies, popping the P then sighing.

She gives him a sympathetic look I'll have to ask her about later, because she stands, making her way up to the big man. She turns and gestures to introduce me. "Dr. Neil Walker, let me introduce you to Nathaniel Black IV."

He holds out his hand. "Of the Black Mountain Blacks?" he asks, and I put my hand in his, giving him a hearty shake to let him know I'm not a little bitch.

"How'd you know?" I ask, slightly worried he knows my family when I'm here to talk about things I'm not quite sure I want them knowing about me.

"I have a cabin on Black Mountain. You stay up that way for even a weekend and you know the history of the place."

I relax a little, understanding he doesn't know them personally. "Yeah, I got picked on in elementary school for all the signs along the trail and for having a museum made out of the first log cabin our ancestors built up there." I reach behind me and rub my neck, giving Evie a half smile when I see her grin at me.

"Because why wouldn't you have a family museum, Mr. Black?" she provokes, and as I lift an eyebrow at her, she has the decency to blush.

"Well, come on in and take a seat," Dr. Walker backs up and allows us into the room, and my eyes go wide at the space. Everything is dark woods and brown leather. There are floor-to-ceiling bookcases along one wall with a huge shiny dark wooden desk that screams power. Directly in front of us is a leather couch, and facing it is a matching chair with a small table next to it that has a notefolio and a pen sitting on top.

Evie walks ahead of me and plops down on the sofa, clearly comfortable in this space that looks absolutely nothing like any therapist's office I've ever been in, and I've been in a lot of them.

"First, let's get this out of the way," he says, opening his folio and handing me the stapled paper that says **Non-Disclosure Agreement** at the top. I look it over quickly, automatically reaching up to my ear and finding the place above it empty. Evie hands me a pen out of her purse with a sweet smile, and I take it with a wink at her before signing my name and putting her pen behind my ear.

"I feel naked, so I'm keeping this," I tell her, and she reaches over to rub my bicep in reassurance.

"Wonderful," Dr. Walker states, sliding the papers back where they came from. "Now. Evelyn told me a little about what's going on. Diagnosed OCD, interest in becoming a Dominant and a member of Club Alias, et cetera. But I'd like to start from the very beginning and hear everything in your words, Nathaniel."

I blow out a breath, hating this part, having to reiterate for what seems like the zillionth time in my life, but I know it needs to happen, and I'm hoping it'll be the last time I'll ever have to do it. "I've been to several therapists and psychiatrists in the past and was diagnosed with Obsessive Compulsive Disorder at the age of eight."

"Symptom dimensions?" he prompts, placing his pad of paper on the arm of his chair and taking down notes as I list them.

"Ah... let's see. Contamination, Symmetry, Arranging and Counting, Doubt and Harm, Unwanted Thoughts, and Rituals. Basically the whole shebang. Oh, and since becoming sexually active when I was fifteen, I feared I had the sexual subtype, but I have a suspicion that it's probably the Dominant thing more than a part of my disorder."

"Genetic or trauma-induced?" he prompts.

"Genetic on my father's side."

Evie shifts on the cushion next to me and makes a T with her hands. "Uuummm... can we take a timeout for a second? I may have a little background in psychology from college, but I haven't gotten far enough to understand everything you two are talking about, and you're going way too fast for me to keep up."

I look over at Dr. Walker, and he gestures for me to explain. "There are four main types of OCD. Contamination is the fear that involves germs, feelings of disgust when it comes to uncleanliness, bodily fluids, sticky substances, and stuff. Symmetry, Arranging, and Counting—"

"That one's a little more self-explanatory. Like the way you have to have your pencils and books just so," she inserts, turning in her seat so she's facing me.

I nod. "Right, but along with that is my compulsion to count. A lot of the time you can't even tell I'm almost always counting in my head. Steps, time—"

"Thrusts," she murmurs, and my eyebrows shoot up at her candidness in front of Dr. Walker. But I guess if he's the one who introduced her to BDSM as a form of therapy years ago, then she's used to talking about sexual things with him. I try to fight back the jealousy that rears its head.

"Oh, you noticed that, did you, mouse?"

"You betcha," she replies with a grin.

I shake my head at her with a smile, realizing I really like this open and comfortable side of her. "Next on the list was Doubt about Accidental Harm and Checking. It's a fear of the possibility of unintentionally harming myself or someone else because I wasn't careful enough or because I was negligent."

"So like when you said you never allowed yourself to be rough with previous sexual partners," she points out, clearly trying to understand and put together everything in her mind.

"Correct. I somehow don't have the Checking part of that subtype, those people you hear about who will unlock and relock the door over and over again, or will turn around and go home when they think they left the stove on. Mine wasn't really anything I could check. I just didn't let myself give in to my desires," I explain, glancing over to see Dr. Walker is taking notes while answering Evie's questions.

"Until me," she replies, pulling my attention back to her.

"Until you." My voice is low, seductive, and I feel myself stiffen behind my zipper at the memories her statement causes.

She swallows, biting her lip, and then purrs, "And I turned out juuust fine."

I clear my throat, continuing on so I don't end up fucking her on this couch in front of the good doctor. "Unwanted thoughts is a big one of mine. This is my intrusive, repetitive thoughts that get stuck in my head and it's hard for me to snap out of it. And then Rituals, which I know you've seen... and experienced."

"The things you do and have to get right the first time or you'll have to start over?" she clarifies.

"Bingo," I tell her, lifting my hand to her face and using my fingertip to push her glasses back up her nose so I can see her beautiful eyes more clearly.

"Can I just say, Evelyn, I've been seeing you for... how many years now?" Doc inserts.

"Um, since my parents passed five years ago," Evie says quietly, and I reach down and take her hand.

"Five years. And while I thought you truly came into your own once you became a member of the club, I have to say I've never seen you so... content, I think is the right word. You seem at peace in Nathaniel's presence," he points out, and I can't help wanting to puff out my chest.

"I feel that way too—well, most of the time at least," she replies, and I deflate a fraction.

"Explain, please?" Dr. Walker prompts.

"Well, I've had a couple near panic attacks when my anxiety got the best of me. He went to go get us lunch, and when it took a while, I almost lost my shit thinking he wasn't coming back."

He makes a note. "And how did that go once he obviously returned, since he's sitting here now?" He points to me when the back end of his pen.

She squeezes my hand. "He immediately recognized what was happening and gave me physical and mental reassurance that he will always come back."

Dr. Walker gives me an approving look before explaining, "Nathaniel, it's important to know that communication will be extremely imperative when getting involved with someone with Evelyn's type of anxiety. Communication is always important in a romantic relationship, of course, but even more so when entering a D/s partnership, and exponentially more when it comes to a person with special needs. Because of the loss of her parents at such an impressionable age, she has abandonment issues we've spent years working through."

I bring her hand up to my lips, kissing her knuckles, an almost unconscious action, and I don't know if I do it to comfort her or to reassure myself that she's okay.

"I'm willing to learn everything I need in order to be worthy of her, whether it's as her Dom or as a regular ol' relationship," I say, looking over at her and giving her a smile. Her face goes soft, and she scoots a little closer to me.

"That's great to hear." He gives us a small smile then looks down at his notes. "Okay, let's get back to you, shall we, Nathaniel?"

"Nate's fine, Dr. Walker," I reply, and he looks up at me, seeming to assess me then glancing down at where Evie clutches my bicep with her hand I'm not holding. He seems to make a decision, and then gives me a nod.

"You can call me Doc as well," he says, and as simple as the exchange would seem to anyone hearing it from the outside, it feels like I just passed a test of some kind, like I'm being welcomed into something... monumental. Evie must understand what I'm feeling, because she rubs my bicep and gives me a great big smile.

"So now that I have a handle on your OCD symptoms, can you tell me what the effects of past therapies had?" Doc prompts.

"Uh, yeah." I clear my throat. "Well, as far as the psychiatrists went, medications were a no-go. SSRIs and antidepressants made me a zombie, anxiolytics made me not want to get out of bed. As far as other treatments, support groups really weren't my thing, aversion therapy made me want to get violent, psychoeducation taught me everything about my disorder but did nothing to treat it, and the list goes on."

"Did anyone try systematic desensitization?" Doc asks, and I go to answer, but Evie interrupts.

"Could you explain that one please? It's the only one I've never heard of."

"It's a form of exposure therapy. It's the process of slowly increasing the sufferer's exposure to their phobias in the hopes that they'll... basically get used to it and not be afraid of it any longer."

"How is that different from aversion therapy?"

"Aversion involves using a painful stimulus to prevent the OCD behavior," I tell her, "at least the version they used on me."

She blinks, searching my face, looking me over as if to see if there were any scars left behind. The look in her eyes does that funny thing to my heart again, making me feel protected and cared for by this tiny woman, when it's *me* who wants to be the one to protect and care for *her*.

"I'm okay, baby," I murmur, feeling the need to reassure her, and her face relaxes a bit, although her mouth still turns down in a little frown that makes me pull her to me a kiss it away, our audience be damned.

When I set her back on her cushion and look up at Doc, he's watching me with an almost amused look on his face. He seems to nod to himself, makes a note, and then before he can say what he opens his mouth to reveal, Evie cries out, "Wait!"

"Yes, Evelyn?" Doc chuckles.

"Sorry, um..." She fidgets with her glasses. "It's just... systematic desensitization. I think... I think we unknowingly might've done that. And I think it worked, even if it was only for a little while."

"How do you mean?" Doc prompts.

She gives me an apologetic look and then turns to face Doc when she explains, "Our first time together, he ummm... he knew I'm a submissive, and I allowed him to uh... let his dominant side out for the first time." She winces, looking like the emoji with all its teeth bared.

Doc stares at her a moment, his face blank before he sets his pen down. "Evelyn. You submitted to an untrained Dominant outside the club?"

She leans back a little on her cushion. "Yeeeaaahhh," she says like a child admitting that she broke a window with her baseball.

His voice changes a little, as if he's no longer a soothing therapist and is now something... different. "Did you inform anyone of your plans before this happened?"

"Mmm..." She lets out high-pitched hum. "Sort of. Dixie knew I was leaving with him." She suddenly gasps, her eyes wide, and she slaps her hand over her mouth. "Shit," she says behind her hand.

My eyes go back and forth between her and the doctor, and then it dawns on me... she had wanted to keep it a secret I had been at the club. My girl can't lie for shit.

"It wasn't her fault." I sit forward, looking the man in his eyes. "She had no idea I was following her. And then I walked into the club and found out what it was."

"Following her." Doc's nostril's flare.

"Yes," I admit without hesitation.

"Stalking her?" He sets his notepad on the table next to him, and I suddenly get the impression I need to explain things quickly and carefully before this guy gets violent. And I'm not foolish enough to think I could take him. The dude has at least fifty pounds of muscle on me.

"It wasn't like that. I thought about her constantly, and not like an OCD intrusive thoughts kind of way, but like a guy who is totally infatuated with a pretty girl kind of way—"

Evie lets out a high-pitched squeak that sounds almost like a giggle but not quite, since she still has her hand over her mouth.

"Anyway, a quick Google search gave me her address..." I turn to her, lowering my brow and say in a scolding voice, "Really need to get you out of the white pages, baby." I turn back to Doc. "...and I showed up to her house just to like... see what she was doing. I thought she'd just be, I don't know, watching TV or something. I really didn't think it through. Didn't think about how crazy I'd look just showing up like that. All I knew was I had to see her. But when I showed up, she was leaving. And I followed her." I deflate a little. "Jesus fuck, I sound like a creeper. Trenton was right."

She makes that awkward giggle sound again, and I shake my head. I've come this far; might as well tell him the rest of it.

"I thought it would be perfect. Maybe she would just be going to a restaurant or something and I could act like I just happened to be running into her. Like, 'Heeey, Ms. Richards. What are you doing here?' I don't know. Some shit like that. But then she puts on some lacy mask around her eyes and disappears behind this super ominous-looking door. So I followed her in. And that's when I discovered what was inside."

"There was no one checking IDs?" Doc growls.

Evie raises her hand. "I got there super early by accident. It... it had been a rough day," she adds, and I wince, knowing it had been me who made her feel that way.

Doc turns his eyes from her back to me. "And how exactly did you know what the club was if she got there before it opened?"

"Kinda put two and two together when I climbed the stairs and saw Ms. Richards standing there in her lingerie," I tell him, my voice flat. And the way his hands fist where his wrists rest on his crossed leg makes me narrow my eyes. "Wait a minute..." I sit back and twist so my back rests against the arm of the couch. "Have..." I look between Doc and Evie, my brows dragging together as the thought that just occurred to me fills me with raging jealousy. "Have you two—"

"No!" Evie cries, but my eyes stay locked with Doc's.

"You were the one who introduced her to this form of 'therapy.' You're part owner of this club. Does that mean you—" I see nothing but red and can't seem to finish that sentence. "I cannot have a therapist who has fucked the woman I—"

Before I know what's happening, Evie is straddling my lap, taking my face in her hands, and forcing me to look into her eyes instead of at Doc, who I want to murder right now even though he's bigger than me. I'm pretty sure there's enough adrenaline in my system right now that I could swing this whole goddamn couch at his fucking head.

"Nathaniel," she murmurs, scooting even closer on my lap to where she's sitting over my hips instead of my thighs. She leans forward and kisses me, and some of the red dissipates. "Baby, I've never been with Doc. And while I might've had a little crush on him when I was seventeen and thought he was super cute—"

I growl, every muscle in my body tensing and ready to attack the fucker.

"—that quickly changed when I started coming to therapy twice a week and I soon saw him more as a father-figure."

I huff. "A father-figure who teaches you BDSM?" I sneer.

"Okay, so not so much a father-figure, but like... the only male I had in my life who taught me how to take care of myself," she explains, and I relax marginally.

I look her in the eyes so I know... I just know she won't be able to lie to me. "He's never once been your Dom?"

"At the club, all submissives respect the Dominants as if they were their own. But if you're asking if we've ever had a scene together, the answer is no."

"I do not scene with my patients," Doc speaks up, his voice calm, and I look over at him, seeing he's picked up his notepad and pen again.

After a moment, I turn back to Evie and give her a slight nod, and she gives me one more quick kiss before sitting back on the couch, albeit keeping her legs over mine and crossing her ankles.

"For the record, Nate, if you decide to become a member of Club Alias, the man you will receive training from to become a Dominant is the same man who taught Evelyn to be a proper submissive."

My eyes snap to his.

"Will you be able to handle knowing the fact that he's scened with your sub?" Doc prompts.

My lips twist while I really think about that question. Could I learn something so important from a man who has fucked my girl? Would I be able to concentrate enough to be trained in this way of life while having the niggling thought in the back of my head, the image of him touching, punishing... *rewarding* the woman who I think of as mine?

Evie speaks up in her sweet voice, and I turn to focus on her. "If it makes a difference, he's now super happily married with a baby on the way. He hasn't touched anyone but her since the day he met her. Seven's a very... hands-off kind of trainer nowadays, but he's still the best around."

That actually does make me feel somewhat better. I'm not one to kiss and tell, but Evie has to know it's some of her own students she sees every day who I fucked in the past. She doesn't seem to let that bother her, so can't I show her the same trust and respect?

I make the decision, knowing this is the path I want my life to take. And if being trained by someone who taught Evie to be such a perfect and amazing submissive, even if that training involved him scening with her, then that's something I'll just have to come to terms with.

"I'll be able to handle it. If it means learning to be the perfect Dom for Evie, I'll do it," I tell them both, and she gives me a beaming smile.

CHAPTER 18

Evie

A little more than two weeks have passed since our first session with Doc. And as per Club Alias membership rules, Nathaniel must go through four sessions with him in order to be assessed thoroughly enough to be cleared to apply to be a member. It's the owners' way of making sure all members of the club are of safe and sound mind before they're let loose to enjoy each other in our private oasis of forbidden fantasies come to life.

We ended the first session not long after Nate's assurance about being trained by Seven, the Dominant in charge of teaching the new Doms and subs about the lifestyle starting from the very basics until they work their way up to big leagues. He also certifies the experienced Doms and subs, so they're able to use all the toys and equipment available in the Club. No one who hasn't been taught is allowed to touch something they haven't been checked off for. We ended the session with Doc assuring me I wouldn't lose my membership for unknowingly leading Nathaniel there, but not before I got a tongue lashing for submitting to an untrained Dom outside the club, to which I had to swear on my future children I would never do again, besides with Nate, who Doc approved of after witnessing how protective he was of me.

In the second and third sessions, we got back on track discussing systematic desensitization, and how we might've been on to that without even knowing what we were doing. By allowing Nate to dominate me, to give in to that side of him that he'd always feared to let loose, it exposed him to the fear, and it allowed him to see he didn't need to be afraid of it. That's why afterward, he didn't have to perform his rituals, why his disorder didn't rule and dictate his actions and mind—because basically he faced his fears and had overcome them.

But since he's had a lifetime of dealing with OCD, doing the systematic desensitization just the one time wouldn't suddenly "cure" him. It would take time and repeated exposure, which I was all too pleased to be of service.

We spent both weekends together, which were just as magical as the first, and it's amazing how close we've gotten in such a short amount of time, spending the entire time from Friday after school until he goes back home Sunday afternoon talking and getting to know every little detail about each other's life in between making love. Although, I do miss my Fridays at Club Alias. It's the atmosphere though, not the company. No... definitely not the company. And I cannot wait until Nathaniel becomes a member and can go with me. Then my life will be complete, combining the best of both worlds.

School days have become like foreplay, riling one another up until we're desperate for each other, so when Friday evening comes along, we're tearing at each other's clothes the moment we get to my house.

It's getting harder and harder to wait, to resist this incredible magnetism between us, which is why, at the end of my day on a Wednesday, I find myself waiting for Nate to get out of swim practice, hidden in the shadows between two sets of lockers. Being the team captain, he told me it's part of his duties to pick up all the equipment and is the last to leave, even after his coach, because he leads the cooldown stretches he and his teammates do at the end of practice.

I hear the loud sounds of teenage boys joking and horsing around as they burst through the doors a ways down before leaving out the set of doors that lead out into the student parking lot. Once all the noise settles down, I then hear the door open once more, along with the jingle of keys, and I peek my head out to see Nate locking the foggy glass doors to the pool.

Sneaking a look up the other end of the hallway, I make sure there are no stragglers, and just as Nate turns to make his way to the exit, I quickly tiptoe up behind him and pinch his butt cheek, letting out a maniacal giggle when he whips around with a "What the fuck!" with a furious scowl on his lips until he sees it's me. I start backing away, a devilish grin on my face.

His instantly morphs, and he lets out a short huff of laughter, and then he's stalking toward me. "You think you're funny, little mouse?" he asks, his voice low and dark. I let out a squeak, spin on my toes, and take off running. I look back as I get to the intersection of hallways, seeing him chase me but not at a run. More like how the killer in a movie hunts their pray at a steady stride and somehow always catches up. But unlike the victims in those movies, I'm careful on my feet and will do all I can not to trip and fall.

With my heart racing and my adrenaline pumping, I turn the corner and sprint toward my library, where I unlocked the door before setting my plan in motion. No students had come in to use the library after school today, so there's no one left, not even the janitor.

I'm hauling ass so fast that I literally skid to a stop in front of the library door, seeing him come around the corner of the darkened hallway and heading in my direction still using his even and long-legged stride. I let out an "Eep!" and shove through the door, running past the circulation desk and toward the wooden staircase leading to the second floor of bookcases. My lungs are screaming and my side is hurting when I'm halfway up the steps, but I push forward and make it to the top before I hear Nathaniel shove through the door.

The lights are all out, but since it's still light outside, the evening sun comes through the wide but short windows along the top of the second story ceiling. I try to steady my breathing, long inhales and exhales through my mouth as I slink in between two rows of book-cases. I grin, hearing Nathaniel climb the stairs, purposely making each step loud as he whistles a tune, playing his part perfectly, even though we hadn't discussed playing any type of game. He just gets me, understands what I want without me having to spell anything out. The perfect Dom to my sub. The yin to my yang.

As quietly as I can, I back up into the darkest shadows, far away from the light coming in through the windows, hearing his whistling getting closer and closer. My heart is pounding inside my chest, but I know it's more from Nathaniel playing this cat-and-mouse game with me instead of the cardio I just got.

"Eeevelyyyn," he singsongs, and I cover my mouth with my palm to keep from giggling, holding my breath and making my lungs feel like they're on fire since they need me to pant for oxygen.

I step back and come up against the wall, my eyes widening at the slight sound, and I try to catch his movement somewhere in front of me.

"I hear you scurrying, little mouse," he says, his sexy, deep voice low and promising wicked things.

I take a breath, still covering my mouth to silence the sound of it, and all I hear is the pounding of my pulse in my ears as I strain to find where he might be.

Everything has gone completely still, the library suddenly seeming eerie, a creepy feeling climbing up my spine and making me shiver. I have no idea where Nathaniel has gone. He never passed by the opening at the far end of this row of bookcases. I would have seen him in the light.

And just as I lower my hand, about to call out his name, I'm suddenly grabbed from the side, Nate's voice rumbling, "Gotcha!" and I squeal as he picks me up. Even though I started this game and know it's my lover who has me midair, my fight-or-flight instinct takes over, my adrenaline rushing throughout my entire body, and I push against him with all my strength, but I'm no match.

It's so dark, and I have the feeling of flying through the air, and suddenly my back is against the wall, Nate's powerful body pressed up against me, and my legs lock around him. I can't see a fucking thing, so I have no time to fight when he takes both my hands and locks my wrists in one of his big mitts above my head.

"This what you want, *Ms. Richards?*" he drawls out my name. "You want the bad guy to chase you and *fuck* you in your library?" With his free hand, he reaches between us, unbuttons and unzips my slacks, and roughly shoves his hand into my panties, immediately sinking two fingers into my embarrassingly wet pussy and making me moan. "Ahhh, yeah. That's exactly what you wanted, my dirty girl," he whispers against my ear, sending a violent shiver throughout my entire body.

He finger-fucks me until I'm circling my hips, fucking myself on his thick digits, until I know my juices have to be drenching his entire hand.

With a growl, he orders, "Unlock your legs," and I do as he says. He lets go of my hands, and I hear rather than see him dropping his pants, so I do the same, vaguely making note that he doesn't even seem to think about his compulsive rituals as he hikes me back up against the wall before I even have a chance to take my panties off. He acts starved for me, as if he can't wait to have me, as if he'll die if he doesn't take me right here and now.

Feeling the fabric blocking his entrance, he reaches between our bodies, takes hold of the crotch of my panties, and rips them away, the elastic digging sharply into my flesh before it snaps, but my blood is fueled with so much passion that the pain feels so good, adding to the desperation I feel for the man now filling me with one smooth, rough thrust of his cock, so deep I feel him slam into my cervix, and I cry out in ecstasy.

My arms come around him, and he takes hold of my thighs with his huge hands. My feet unlock as he uses his immeasurable strength to hold me up and fuck me against the wall of my library. No... not my library. Not my cute little library I have at home, safe where no one can find us. No.

The academy's library.

His family's academy's library.

Where I work.

Where he's a student.

Where my student, my lover, pounds his long, thick, steely cock into me over and over until I'm crying out with each thrust. Because he's not holding back. He's not keeping his control contained like he always did before me. He's giving me everything he's got, and while he's fucking into me, he's whispering things in my ear, dirty things, sweet things, promises that he's never going to let me go, that I'm the only one he'll ever want.

And I come. I come so long and hard that I can't breathe as I let out a silent scream the entire length of my orgasm.

And if it weren't for the feminine voice at the other end of the bookcase calling out "Ms. Richards, you okay?" I would've been lost to subspace once again.

But I'm not. Instead of floating above my body in blissful near-unconsciousness, I'm staring down the now lit tunnel of books into the face of my biggest nightmare.

Because me and my student, my lover, have been caught.

CHAPTER 19

Nate

My eyes are closed as I pour my heart and soul into the words I whisper against Evie's ear while I thrust in and out of her tight, wet heat. The excitement, the adrenaline of playing this lovers' game she initiated was the key that unlocked all the feelings and things I've kept inside, everything that's built up over the months I taunted her, and then the last several weeks in which we both gave in to our every desire. With every night she's slept in my arms, with every time we've made love, with every study hour we've spent having to keep our true feelings hidden, with every stolen kiss between these very bookcases, with every session we've spent in Doc's office, and with the hours upon hours of staying up late at night, talking on the phone, texting, even FaceTiming, we've grown closer than I ever imagined two people could be. Close enough that I know what I feel for Evelyn Richards is love. Undeniable, untouchable love.

And I'm confessing everything, telling her all the things I feel for her, my eyes squeezed tight as Evelyn's pussy clamps around me as she comes, yanking me along to base jump right off the cliff with her.

So I don't see the moment the lights overhead flip on. I only hear the voice mere seconds after I fill Evie with every drop of cum I have.

"Ms. Richards, you okay?"

I know that voice, and right now, I've never hated anyone more in my entire life, because I know she's not going to let this go. The girl can't keep a secret to save her life.

Without turning around, I lower Evie until her feet touch the floor, and I tuck myself back into my underwear, pulling my pants back up my legs, a part of me recognizing I hadn't even thought to bother with my undressing ritual, and grateful I had wanted Evie so desperately that I didn't undress all the way. Because it makes this a fraction less humiliating. I'm able to keep Evelyn hidden with my big body, because unlike mine, her pants and shoes are on the floor a foot away. Her panties are ripped and lying at our feet. I spin around, keeping Evelyn's nudity concealed as I face the intruder, the person who just ruined the greatest, most epic moment of my entire life.

Lindy lifts her brows in surprise then crosses her arms over her cheerleading-uniform-covered chest as she pops her hip.

"Really, Nate?" Her voice is acidic, eating through this perfect bubble Evie and I have been wrapped in for the last three and half weeks. "Is that the reason you keep telling me no? Didn't want me again, because you're slumming it with a teacher?"

I take a step forward, but Evie grabs my arm, keeping me in place, and it reminds me I need to keep her blocked from Lindy's ugly sneer. The woman I love doesn't need to see the look this bitch is trying to give her.

But the look I give Lindy makes that expression slide right off her face, and she drops her arms, taking a step back. And when a deep, dark, almost terrifying growl rumbles throughout the bookshelves, Lindy takes off out of sight and down the staircase before I even realize the sound was coming from me.

I turn back around, picking up Evie's pants and holding them open for her to step into when I see she's trembling so badly she can't even move.

"Oh God," she says on an exhale, and her knees buckle just as I'm buttoning her slacks. I catch her against me, sliding us both to the floor so I can put her shoes on her feet, snatching up her torn panties and shoving them in my pocket before I stand up with her in my arms.

"It's going to be fine, baby," I promise her, carrying her down the stairs, and she bursts into tears.

"This is all my fault," she wails, and her wracking sobs break my heart.

I shake my head. "It's not—"

"It is!" she cries. "You didn't do this. You've been so careful, so aware, even warning me when you thought I was acting in a way someone might get suspicious. And what did I do? I lured you into the library at school to have sex!" She can't catch her breath after that. And I move faster once I realize she's starting to have a panic attack, knowing I have to snap her out of it.

I set her on the circulation desk and force her to look into my eyes. The fear and misery in hers gut me, but I know I have to be strong for her. "Evelyn," I say, my tone deep, commanding, "this is not your fault. And as my sub, I demand you trust that I will take care of this."

She whimpers, shaking her head frantically as she tries to take a deep breath, the tears streaming down her cheeks.

"Do you truly believe I'd let anything happen to you? Do you really think I'll allow anyone to ruin your life, to ruin what we have together?" I prompt rhetorically, asking the questions as a reminder that I told her before I'd hurt anyone who tried to come between us, who tried to hurt Evie in any way.

Just when my words finally cut through her panic, before I can say anything else to dissipate her overwhelming worry, the doors of the library burst open, and Lindy walks in... along with the assistant principal, Mr. Moran.

"See?" Lindy gestures toward us dramatically, as if the man didn't immediately spot me holding Evie to my chest while she sat on the desk, me between her legs. But I don't give a shit. My woman comes above everything and everyone else. It's my job to take care of her, and I don't give a fuck who sees it.

Mr. Moran clears his throat. "Uh... thank you, Lindy. Please, drive home safe," he says, dismissing her, clearly uncomfortable seeing Evie and me in this position.

She gives a theatrically bratty huff as she stomps her foot, and then she marches out the door.

Mr. Moran reaches up to rub his bald head for a second, looking everywhere but at me while I continue to hold Evie, rubbing circles along her back as I focus on the assistant principal's eyes. He never meets mine, but he says with a sigh, "Well... come with me, you two. Gotta call your parents, kid."

Evelyn jerks, and my arms tighten around her. "It'll be okay, baby," I tell her once more, and I slide her off the desk and set her on her feet, wrapping an arm around her to keep her steady as we walk to the office.

CHAPTER 20

Evie

It's my worst nightmare come to life. How could I have been so stupid? How had I let my lust and desire overrule my mind and ruin my own freaking life? In the beginning of all this, I had been so worried Nathaniel would blackmail me, tell everyone about my private life, how I was a member of a BDSM club. And then later, I was worried his flirtations would make it obvious there was something going on between us. But no. It was me, it was my own stupid self who couldn't just wait two more freaking days to make love with Nate, to wait until Friday when we could be in the privacy of my sanctuary, my home, without worry of being caught. Just two more days, and we could've had another weekend spending every moment together, wrapped up in each other, where the rest of the world disappeared and all that was left was us.

No. It was me who got him to chase me into the library, me who made it perfectly clear I wanted him to fuck me right then and there.

"I... I thought we were the only ones here," I tell Nate as we trail behind Mr. Moran, and he tightens his grip around my shoulders.

"Cheerleaders practice late during football season, baby," he replies, and I feel like an idiot. Of course they do. If I paid any sort of attention to my students' extracurriculars, if I cared even the slightest to support all the school's sports and our athletes, I would've remembered that. But no, I'm a horrible teacher. All I care about on Friday nights is getting home as fast as I can so I can get ready to go to my BDSM club, not giving one shit about the kids' football games and other things that are important to them during their high school career.

We follow Mr. Moran into the main office and then through the reception area to enter his. He gestures toward the chairs across from him as he rounds the desk, sitting down and pulling his phone close to him.

And then I lose time. I'm vaguely aware of the two males speaking back and forth. I even manage to acknowledge it when Nathaniel asks if I'm all right. But I'm fairly certain I skip right past my panic attack and just black out, even though I somehow stay upright in my seat.

It's not until I hear other people enter the office from behind me—Nate's parents, I assume—that I snap back to the here and now, and without thinking, I shoot out of my seat, spin around, and back away from them. I don't know if it's because I think his mother might launch at me and choke the life out of me for sleeping with her precious only son, or if it's something else that sets off my fight-or-flight, but while the instinct needle had flipped to the fight side earlier, when Nathaniel had caught me in the library, it most certainly was pointing all the way in the red, alarms going off inside my head for me to fucking fly.

But there's nowhere to run. And so I don't look like a complete freaking moron, I gesture to my now empty seat, saying to the beautiful woman with chestnut hair and big doe eyes the same color as her son's, "Please, sit." It's then I realize I've backed myself into a corner, and I don't know whether I feel trapped, or if I feel safer since nothing can come at me from the back.

"Oh, thank you, sweetheart," she replies and sits, and her voice is so sweet, so pleasant-sounding, and it breaks my heart to think that it's going to sound so very different when she hears why she's here. This woman, who Nate painted such a wonderful image of in my mind, the best mom, the Pinterest mom, the woman his dad married for true love. I'd fantasized about meeting her in the future, about what it'd be like to have a close relationship with her, since I no longer have a mother of my own. She had been as much of a dream as Nate was, and now I'm going to lose it all.

Nate stands as well and offers his dad the chair, and his dad glances at me, asking silently if I want to take the now open seat—a gentleman, like his son.

"No thank you," I reply, my voice trembling, and Mrs. Black's face falls a little when she hears it.

Nathaniel comes to stand next to me, and as if he isn't aware that his parents are right here, staring at us, as if we are on stage and in a spotlight, he wraps his arms around me and pulls me to his chest. I stiffen, my eyes going wide, and I start to struggle away, but he just tightens his grip, bending down to press a kiss to the top of my head and whispering a "Shhh" against my hair. "Trust me."

Mr. Moran clears his throat yet again, and all I can do is watch this train wreck happen, unable to look away with Nate trapping me in my front row seat. "Mr. and Mrs. Black, let me start by saying this is incredibly awkward for me. Obviously, seeing as this academy is your family's legacy, and I am an employee of yours. Also, because Nathaniel is a star student. He's never had to be disciplined in any way, always the epitome of what a pupil should be."

I can't help but snort at that, knowing damn well I tried to turn him in for basically harassing me and was shut down before the words could even leave my mouth. And then I yelp when Nate reaches down and pinches my ass, horrified when everyone turns my way in confusion at what probably looks on the outside like I have Tourette's. Thankfully, Mr. Moran just continues.

"I must inform you that a student came upon your son and Ms. Richards in a... compromising position in the library."

Mrs. Black eyes widen, and her mouth drops open just a little, her cheeks turning bright pink. Mr. Black reaches over and takes her hand, but his expression doesn't change except to lift a brow at his son.

"As your son is eighteen, he is a consenting adult. In our state, there is no statutory rape case here. But... there are ethical considerations to be made. There is a policy in place at our school to punish faculty to protect students, since their parents have entrusted their children with them. You may choose to press charges against Ms. Richards that will take away her teaching certification," he tells them, and I sink against Nate, Mr. Moran's words taking the life right out of me.

Nate's arm comes up to pull my head against his chest, and I shut my eyes, forcing myself to absorb the sound of his strong but steady heartbeat against my ear. How can he be so calm at a time like this? How can his pulse be so smooth when mine feels like I'm having a full-on heart attack? It almost makes me mad, him being so cool and collected. I mean, it's not *his* life that hangs in the balance. But I thought he'd at least be worried for mine, especially after all the things he said to me in the library not forty-five minutes ago.

And then I flinch back at the sound of Mrs. Black's gentle voice that is so close to me, so close she could attack me for corrupting her "perfect" son. But when I register her words, recognize she's not speaking to me but to Nate in a tone I fully didn't expect, I crack one eye open.

"So this is your little mouse, my boy?" she asks him, no smile on her lips but her eyes are twinkling, and my brow furrows in confusion.

"It is," he replies, his voice proud, and her eyes look down from his towering height over both of us until she's looking straight ahead into mine. For some reason, my body relaxes when she stays there, seeming to read me, seeming to tell me something with her beautiful doe eyes, and Nate unfurls his hand from the back of my head so I can stand up straighter, still in his arms. A moment later, Mrs. Black gives me the smallest smile, and she turns back to the assistant principal.

"That won't be necessary, Mr. Moran. I'll sign whatever waiver I need in order to give my consent to this relationship," she tells him, and I gasp, looking from her, to her husband—who has a little smirk on his lips as he looks at his son that looks oh-so familiar—then up to Nate, who is, in fact, giving me that same damn look as he stares down at me.

A thousand whirling thoughts overwhelm my mind, but only one thing comes out of my mouth when I see that expression. "You told your parents about me?" I squeak.

He lets out a cocky laugh. "Didn't I tell you not to worry, that you should trust me?"

I open and close my mouth like a fish, not knowing how to answer that. There's activity inside the assistant principal's office, shuffling of papers, things being signed, and hands being shaken. I vaguely hear Mr. Moran assuring Nathaniel's schedule wouldn't have to be altered since I'm not technically one of his teachers in a graded class, and then I'm moving as Nate leads me toward the door.

"Evelyn, dear. Would you do us the honor of coming for dinner tonight? I know you commute quite far, but I've already got it in the oven, so you'll still be able to head home at a decent hour," Mrs. Black invites, and I'm startled that she already knows that much about me.

My lips reply before my head even catches up. "I'd love to."

"You've been through a lot, baby. You'll ride with me and I'll bring you back to your car once you're good and full and your nerves aren't as frazzled," Nate informs me, and I close my eyes, grateful to have finally found my Dominant half and he's chosen this moment to assert it.

"That's sounds perfect," I tell him, and even though his mom is right there watching us, I can't help but tip my head up to give him an appreciative smile, to which he leans down, just like I knew he would, and places a sweet kiss to my lips.

My cheeks flame, even though I know I instigated it, and I shyly meet his mother's eyes. But all I see there is the twinkle of happiness, not the look of a woman luring me back to her home to kill me slowly for defiling her precious only child.

"Let's go grab your things, little mouse," Nate tells me, and we turn to make our way down the hallway as his dad calls out.

"Takes eight minutes and thirteen seconds to get to our house, son. Better see you there in fifteen."

And my hand slaps over my mouth as I let out a giggle—one, because his dad was clearly stating there was to be no more shenanigans in the library, and two, because it sounded so very like something Nate would say.

CHAPTER 21

Evie

On the ride to his house, Nate seems to sense I need a minute to process everything that just happened, so he holds my hand and turns up his music, giving me the time to get my thoughts in order. And just like his dad said, with a glance at the clock in Nathaniel's fancy dashboard, I see it only took eight minutes to get here. I look out the windshield at the sprawling... I can't even call it a house. It's a freaking mansion if I've ever seen one, and Nate laughs at the first thing that comes out of my mouth.

"You said your mom does everything herself? She must clean from sunup to sundown."

"Nah, we have housekeepers, but Mom cooks and does all the decorating and stuff herself. She's a homemaker minus the maidly duties," he explains, and I nod, my eyes never leaving the freaking castle before me.

"She's living the good life," I murmur, and he chuckles.

"Let's go in before my dad has an aneurism because I'm late."

I scoff. "You mean before you have an aneurism for being late."

"Tomatoes, to-mah-toes." He gets out and comes around the hood, opening my door and leaning across me to unbuckle my seatbelt as always. Something I've never questioned, since it makes me feel so taken care of. I place my hand in his and he helps me down from his truck, and then he leads me up the steps to the giant front doors, my eyes trying to take everything in at once.

The door opens just as he reaches for the knob, startling me a bit, especially when I see his mom standing there with an expression I can't quite decipher. But I take it as excitement when suddenly she grips me by the shoulders and hauls me over the threshold and into a tight hug. It all happens so fast I stand there stiffly for a second, but then Nathaniel's "Mooom, stop suffocating my girl" echoes throughout the huge foyer, and I relax against her, bringing my arms up to lay my palms flat against the middle of her back. She's shaped a lot like me, petite and thin, but her hips are a little wider and she's got about an inch of height on me. Her scent is a pleasant floral.

She feels like home.

When she finally pulls back, Nate closes the door behind us, and she brings her palms up to cup my jaw for a moment before grasping my upper arms gently. "Let me look at you. Oh, how I've been dying to meet you," she confides, and I glance up at Nate nervously as he circles to stand behind his mom. "You're right, my boy. She's absolutely lovely," she tells him over her shoulder, and my face flames.

"Thank you," I whisper, still not quite registering what's happening right now, and I lift my hand to push my glasses up my nose just to have something to do with my hands.

"Come, sweet girl. You can help me plate the food while Nate goes and showers," she says, linking her arm with mine and pulling me to the right. But Nathaniel speaks up.

"I'll just shower later, after I take Evie back to her car. I'll set the table, Mom," he replies and walks ahead of us. Mrs. Black stops, her arm tightening through mine, and brings me to a halt, and when I look over at the woman, her mouth is dropped open, and I see tears fill her eyes. She turns the look on me then closes her mouth, blinking back the tears and letting out a little laugh.

"I don't know what you did, sweet girl, but thank you. Thank you

A LESSON IN BLACKMAIL

for healing whatever it was inside him that his father and I and countless doctors never could," she says in a low tone, and she pulls me in for another hug that I melt into. When she stands back up, she seems to shake off the thick emotions, gives me a big grin, and pulls me along to the kitchen, which is straight out of a freaking lifestyle magazine.

Nate is washing his hands in the giant trough-style sink, and I watch him curiously, noting that he no longer seems to count inside his head. He doesn't wash them rigorously a certain number of times front and back and between his fingers. He just... soaps up, looking over his shoulder to wink at me, rinses them after several seconds, and then turns off the faucet, snatching off a random number of paper towels instead of counting them out like he did once before at my house, and dries them, tossing the towels into the garbage on his way to pull open the silverware drawer. And then he disappears into what must be the dining room.

Mrs. Black chuckles softly beside me. "My water bill thanks you too," she whispers, and it startles a snort out of me. As if these people have to worry about their bills being high. They look like they could afford to run the Niagara Falls.

Twenty minutes later, I'm next to Nathaniel at a six-seated dining room table, his mom and dad across from us. I was surprised at the intimate setting, expecting the table to stretch for a mile with a countless number of seats, and Nate picked up on it without me saying a word.

"This is our family dining room. The formal has a table that seats forty," he informed me, and I pulled my lips between my teeth before whispering to him, "Of course it does."

"So, Evelyn," his dad says, laying his napkin across his lap and turning his plate a fraction of an inch, a move so similar to something I've seen Nathaniel do with his pencils and books that it's endearing if I were to ignore the fact that it's an actual disorder that causes him to need things to be just right. "Nate has told us so much about you—all of it good, so don't worry." He says it sincerely instead of flippantly, as if my anxiety is something Nathaniel also informed him of, and he wants to reassure me before I have time to overthink it.

I smile appreciatively at him, instantly warming to him. "He's told me wonderful things about the two of you too. Yet he seemed to leave out the part that you knew about me," I reply, turning my head and lifting a brow at him. "Although, I have to admit I'm grateful he did."

Nate leans over and kisses my cheek before turning back to his plate, and everyone digs in. It's all way more relaxed than I imagined it would be; everyone has table manners, but it's not the scene out of *The Princess Diaries* I thought I would be stepping into, where I'd play the role of the clueless Mia while she tries to fake her way through using the proper utensils. There's only one fork, one spoon, and a steak knife next to each of our plates. There's even a community butter knife set on top of the big plastic tub of butter in the center of the table. I stare at it for a moment, finding it weird when we're sitting in the largest estate in Black Mountain. Shouldn't the butter be in perfect little pallets in some fancy dish? Especially in a house full of men who literally fear imperfection?

"My momma was a nurse, and my dad was a miner, sweet girl. This house is a mix of my meager beginnings and *my* Nathaniel's fancy upbringing," Mrs. Black tells me, easily reading my unspoken wonderings.

I smile at her across the table. "That has to get pretty confusing, in a house with men who all have the same name."

She laughs and shakes her head. "No, Dad is Nathaniel, and son is Nate. It just makes life a lot easier around here," she explains.

"Noted," I say, relaxing a bit knowing she came from the same humble background as I did. "I am curious though. How..." I side-eye Nate. "How did you first learn about me exactly?"

"Well," she begins, "at first there were subtle differences in Nate himself. He started complimenting me on things he never had before—"

"Sorry, Mom," Nate inserts, sounding guilty.

"Oh, hush, honey. What teenage boy is going to remember to tell his mother how great her cooking is every day? It was just a nice and noticeable difference that just suddenly began out of nowhere. And then more obvious things, like his OCD symptoms lessening day by day," she explains, and I nod, knowing what she means by that. "And *then*—" Her voice rises on the word, and she smiles over at her husband, who winks at her as he chews. "—the insurance claim letter came from a Dr. Neil Walker in a town an hour away from here."

My eyes widen, and I look over at Nate, who just chuckles. "Yeah, didn't even think about that, baby. I am only eighteen, after all," he murmurs, and I choke on my water I just lifted to my mouth. He laughs, rubbing my back, and I swat at him.

Mrs. Black is smiling ear-to-ear when I look up again. "So when we asked Nate about it, he started spilling everything."

"Everything?" I squeak, turning wide eyes to Nate then back to her.

"Everything!" his mom says loudly through a giggle at the same time Nate whispers so only I can hear, "*Not* everything, mouse." And I relax a bit.

"He said he had met someone he had real feelings for. Which alone would've made my day, seeing as our son has always claimed not to have any." She shakes her head at him. "And then he told us about your own anxiety disorder and how medications and such never worked for you, just like him, but this one therapist you've been seeing for years used a method that finally succeeded in helping you. He said he agreed to go with you to check him out, and might I say, whatever that man is doing in that office is miracle work. Hell, I might have to go check him out myself!" she chirps, and I choke on the roll I just took a bite of.

"Sweet girl, you sure seem to be having a hard time eating. You feeling all right? What happened back in the assistant principal's office isn't still messing with your nerves, is it? I get a nervous belly too, but I promise you've got nothing to worry about as far as that stuff goes. We won't let anything happen to the woman who has changed our son's life for the better," Mrs. Black says, and my heart warms at her caring tone. I just can't tell her that no, I don't have a nervous belly; I was just startled by the image of Nate's parents showing up at Club Alias.

Not that Doc would ever let that happen. He'd never reveal the form of therapy that's truly working on Nate and me, except to maybe disclose that it's technically systematic desensitization, but nothing about the BDSM side of things.

"I truly appreciate that, Mr. and Mrs. Black. This is my dream job, and I... I didn't mean to get involved with one of my students. He just—"

"Oh, we know, Evie. He told us how he wooed you until you finally could no longer resist his charms and agreed to go on one secret date with him. He promised that if you didn't want to see him again, he would leave you alone and never tell anyone about it at school," she interrupts, and I slowly turn my head to meet the eyes of the scoundrel next to me as his nostrils flare, mischief filling his eyes as he tries to hold back his laughter. Mrs. Black continues on. "I can tell you right now, honey. *No one* can resist the charms of the Black men. Trust me, I tried."

Mr. Black clears his throat. "But that's a story for another day, my love," he inserts, finally getting a word in with his sweet but chatty wife.

I face forward once again.

"Anyway," his mom says, seeming only to be able to stay silent long enough to take a bite of food and swallow it. God, how I love her already. "He told us about you. At first, it was just things like what you looked like, how you were a few years older than him—which I was actually grateful for. The girls around here that are his age are spoiled little bitches." I squeak out one startled laugh as Mr. Black scolds her gently, but she waves him off. "You know they are, Nathaniel. He said that you were a librarian and owned your own home in the town on the insurance claim. Told us about your parents." Her voice is low for that last part, and I see sympathy in her eyes. "Yet it wasn't the *things* he was telling us about you, but *how* he was saying them, like you were this angel sent to him, and he was so... just... smitten." She ends with a dreamy smile. "And let me tell you, I have only seen one other man in this entire family ever be *smitten*." She turns toward her husband and makes a goofy face at him.

"Definitely smitten kitten, my love," he admits unashamedly, and he leans over to give a soft and quick kiss to her lips. I feel my face get warm but not out of embarrassment at their PDA. I've been a member of Club Alias long enough to not give one flip about any type of PDA. I feel warm because of the love I see between the two of them, and how he's looking at her the way Nate always looks at me.

"He just failed to mention that you are, in fact, the librarian at the school," she adds, and my face does flush with embarrassment then, since they know exactly what we were doing in the school library. At my blush, she giggles, reaching out for the butter knife and pulling the tub toward her. "So how about... my only request... is if you two want a little alone time, make sure it's in the privacy of your home and not where anyone could just... stumble upon you in a compromising position." She quotes Mr. Moran's awkwardness and grins over at Mr. Black, and if a hole would open up and swallow me beneath the table, I'd gladly dive in headfirst.

I clumsily agree to her request, with a silent addendum about places where people have been legally sworn to secrecy.

CHAPTER 22

Nate

Today feels different.

After all the excitement from yesterday evening, from the moment Evie surprised me in the hallway, to the mind-blowing sex we had in the library, to getting caught and sent to the principal's office, right down to the moment after we ate, when my crazy mom hugged her goodbye and wouldn't let her go for a full minute, making Evie promise she'll make it at least a weekly habit to come over for dinner before she released her to me, the whole world just feels... different.

There's a lightness inside me, but at the same time, I feel fuller. Like I'm complete. And as I sit in the library watching my woman flit around putting away books and helping other students, I realize I never once checked my watch today to count down the minutes. It's like, once everything between us was out in the open, I felt secure, secure in our relationship, so I didn't have that urgency to get to her and see for myself she still wanted me. I still looked forward to seeing her as much as I ever did, it was just... different. A less maniacal necessity.

It didn't take long for the entire senior class to hear about what Lindy had seen. She wasted no time spreading it through the cheerleading squad, who told the football team, and then it spread exponentially from there. So when I got to school, that's all anyone wanted to talk to me about.

Good. Let the rumor spread to the ends of the earth. Let everyone know that the hot librarian at our school is fucking *mine*.

I was actually able to concentrate in class; therefore, I didn't have any schoolwork to finish up in study hall. So in order to keep from following Evie around like a lost puppy, I sink back in my chair and crack open the latest Stephen King novel, which she had sitting in my spot at the table when I came in. I looked up to find her watching me when I spotted it, and it took everything in me not to stride over to the circulation desk and kiss her for the thoughtful gift.

Which brings me to now, two chapters in and tuning out the chatter around me. Lindy had been smart enough not to sit next to me, but she's still at my table, just at the far end. I don't hear exactly what she says, but I hear her mention Evie's name, and I look up to where my woman is at the circulation desk once again, and I see she's listening to the bitch at my table.

That's when I decide to tune in to what's being said.

"...could have anyone he wants, including me, and he chooses her?" She scoffs snottily. "I just don't get it. She's not even that pretty."

My nostrils flare, and my eyes turn to Lindy, who's facing Jamie beside her. Jamie has the decency to look uncomfortable as she glances over at me, but Lindy keeps on running her mouth, not realizing I've started paying attention to their one-sided conversation.

"I mean, what's she got that I don't have? Who is she compared to me? What makes that... nerdy *freak* so special?" Lindy asks, my eye's drilling into her, and suddenly the room goes red.

But just as my legs go tense and my chair loudly scoots back across the floor, an echoing, startling bang reverberates throughout the library, causing the girls at the table to scream and jump back in their seats. My eyes turn away from the stupid cunt on the end to see my woman directly in front of me, slightly bent at the waist as her hands brace on the table. The sound had obviously come from her slamming the giant hardcover tome down on the table. She's staring at Lindy with a dark look I've never seen on her beautiful face before, and I'm not ashamed to admit my cock goes instantly hard.

"I may not be some supermodel," Evelyn says, and if it weren't for being stunned immobile by the tone and the image she makes, I'd interrupt that self-deprecating sentence. Instead, I watch my woman speak in a way I never thought she had in her. "I might not drive a fancy car, or live in a mansion, or spend thousands of dollars on a pair of shoes."

Lindy comes out of her shock and haughtily crosses her arms over her chest, making a stupid-looking duck face.

"I might have never been a cheerleader, or popular, or the girl everyone wanted to *smash*," Evie continues, and Trenton whistles next to me. "But I am not a *freak*," she says low, her chin tipping down as she stares at Lindy over the rim of her glasses. "And I'm proud of what I *am*, Ms. Jones."

Lindy tries to look like she's unaffected, but I can tell by the way her fingers grip her bicep that she's embarrassed someone is calling her on her shit for once, and in front of everyone, no less. "Oh yeah? And what's that?" she questions, putting extra attitude behind it to hide her discomfort.

Evelyn smiles darkly then stands up straight, gesturing to all the bookcases surrounding us, her eyes following her hand. "I... am a *librarian*," she answers boastfully. And then her hands come back down on the table as she meets Lindy's eyes once more. And just when I think that's the end of her speech, she lifts a finger and points directly at me. "And I. Belong. To *him*."

Out of my peripheral vision, I see Lindy's jaw drop at the same time Trenton slaps me on my back, but it's the stunning creature before me, who spins gracefully and sashays back to the circulation desk who has my full and undivided attention. And just to make it perfectly clear, as if there was any doubt left in anyone's mind, I call loudly across the room.

"I love you, Ms. Richards!"

I see her blush from here. "I love you too, Mr. Black."

And then the bell rings.

CHAPTER 23

Evie

I see Lindy gather her things quickly and storm out of the library, everyone else chattering quietly about what just happened. As all the other students file out of the room, Nate pushes in all the chairs as always then puts his hands in his pockets and strolls up to my desk. I meet him from the other side, the three feet of wood still separating us. My adrenaline is still running high after the confrontation, but I can't hide the smile on my face.

He leans down, propping his elbows on the desk, taking my hand between his. "*The Mummy*, Evie?"

I giggle. "I've always wanted to use that line."

He grins. "Funny you're a librarian named Evie. I never thought about it before."

"It's my all-time favorite movie. She's the whole reason I ever wanted to become one in the first place," I confide, shivering when he runs a fingertip down the center of my palm before lifting it to his lips and placing a kiss there.

"You know, that movie came out before I was even born." He lifts a brow.

I snort. "You say that like I was *that far* behind you."

"I'm just sayin'," he replies, standing to his full height. "Only one more day."

My breath catches at the heat in his eyes. "Only one more day," I echo breathlessly, knowing that tomorrow is Friday and another weekend begins. And all the things he could possibly plan to do to me fill my mind.

"See you later, little mouse," he murmurs, kissing my knuckles before backing away.

All I do is nod, unable to speak as he gives me such a hungry and promising look.

The following Tuesday, Nate and I sit in Dr. Walker's office for his final session. The first thing out of my mouth when we sat down though was to retell the story of me taking up for myself in the library last Thursday, which led to Nate having to backtrack and tell him everything that happened last week, starting with the game I initiated.

While I did get scolded for my poor choice in setting, Doc was proud of me for both situations. He pointed out that, even though I'm a submissive, that shouldn't stop me from doing the things I want in life. I don't have to let every decision be made for me, and if there's something I want, I should never be afraid to voice it and make it happen. He also made sure Nathaniel rewarded me for sticking up for myself, which he most certainly did... thrice.

He enjoyed the story of me meeting Nate's family and how it had been Doc in a roundabout way who shed light on our relationship to his parents, since it had been his office's insurance claim. And he was excited that the Blacks were so supportive of us.

Which leads us to now.

"Well, Nathaniel, I believe I can agree that with proper training you will make a great Dominant and member of Club Alias. Mind you, the first several months are probationary. After you fill out the membership forms and pay your fee, I'll include my letter of approval. Evelyn will be your sponsor, so be on your best behavior—at the very least, for her sake. This includes when you meet your trainer Seven. Understand?" Doc prompts with a stern look.

Nate holds up both hands in surrender. "All good, Doc. Evie made it loud and clear to the whole world that she belongs to me, so I'll be fine."

I slap his abs with the back of my hand, but he doesn't even flinch. "It was one study hall group, not the whole world." I roll my eyes.

"Mouse, you could've said it to one *person*, and it would've spread through the school like wildfire," he points out, and I purse my lips.

"Fair enough," I grumble, and he wraps his arm around me and tucks me into his side.

"So uh, Doc. How do I get this ball rolling? It's Tuesday, and while my girl hasn't said anything about it, I know she's anxious to be back in her 'happy place,' as she calls it, and I was hoping to take her there this Friday," Nate tells him, and I perk up, my eyes going wide at the possibility.

Doc nods, making a note on his pad. "I'll make sure to expedite your paperwork if you want to get me everything by tomorrow."

"I'll call my accountant tonight," Nate replies, and I snort next to him. When he turns his head to look at me with a raised brow, I pull my lips between my teeth. "What?" he prompts.

I shake my head. "Nothing," I singsong, but when he tickles my side, I squeal. "First, a financial advisor, and now an accountant. You're the oldest eighteen-year-old I've ever known."

"Can't let you feel like too much of a cradle robber," he teases, and I squawk and punch his side… to which he doesn't even flinch… again.

"Well, you two, that's the end of your hour," Doc says, setting his pad to the side and standing. He holds his hand out to Nate when we stand from the couch, and he grips it tightly. "While the average number of sessions for club entry is four, and I've approved you for membership, I'd like to suggest you continue coming, maybe twice a month, for a session for us to keep an eye on your OCD, just until we really get a handle on the symptoms and to document how your Dominant training effects it."

"Will do, Doc. I'll be here," Nate agrees, and I beam up at him. "Will you be at the club on Friday?"

"I haven't decided yet. I have... other things I'm working on at the moment, but I might stop by just to say hi," Doc replies, and he pulls out some papers from his folio. "Here's the membership application and the account information for the money transfer."

"Sounds good. I'll get it sent ASAP."

And with that, we leave the office, and Nathaniel takes me out for a nice dinner, claiming he wants a steak. Two hours later, we go to my house for a "celebratory quickie," as he calls it, before he tucks me into bed and heads home.

CHAPTER 24

Nate

There's so much to look at, but at the same time, all I see is Evelyn. Dressed in black lace lingerie, a sheer black robe wrapped around her to make me a little less homicidal, I can't stop looking at her. Somehow, she transformed the moment she stepped into the club. Still submissive and respectful, but every last drop of her anxiety and unconscious fidgeting—gone. Gone is my little, meek library mouse, and in her place is a sensual cougar who reeks of confidence. I've had a perma-boner since the moment we arrived.

And although there are countless women around in various states of undress, it's not even a challenge to pay sole attention to the woman I love, because she's the most beautiful of them all.

We sit in one of the large black leather booths, Evie sipping a glass of white wine while I finish off my mineral water. Just because I'm now a member of an elite BDSM club doesn't mean I get to illegally drink underage. Not that I would anyway, since I drove, and I wouldn't risk putting my girl in any type of unnecessary danger.

Evie perks up beside me. "Oh! There he is! Awww, look at her little belly," she coos, and I turn in the direction she's looking.

"That's the trainer? Seven or whatever?" I prompt, looking him up and down, allowing myself just one moment to imagine him with Evelyn. My nostrils flare with jealousy, but then the couple approaches a guy who would tower over even *me*.

"Yes, and the Dom they're talking to is called Knight," she tells me. "And before you ask, no, I've never scened with him. He never participated in the activities here until recently, when he too got married and his wife started coming. Interesting relationship those two have."

"How so?" I ask curiously.

"They're switches."

"Switches?" I prompt, my brow furrowing, unfamiliar with the term. I haven't come across it in my research.

She leans her head on my shoulder, but I continue to watch the three near the bar. "Yeah, they switch roles. Sometimes he's the Dom, and then the other times *she* is."

I huff. "Don't get any ideas, mouse."

She scoffs. "As if. Could you imagine?" She giggles.

I chuckle. "No, I can't."

I stare at the trainer as they all chat for a minute, and then Seven turns to his wife, places his hands gently on either side of her little bump, and proceeds to bend down and loudly motorboat her tits. I lift a brow at that then watch as his wife laughs and swats him away, shaking her head as she looks back up at the tall dude while Seven steps behind her, wrapping his arms around her and placing his chin down on her shoulder. When he starts swaying their bodies back and forth to the beat of the music filling the club, rubbing big circles on her belly with open palms, I look away just as she closes her eyes and he places a kiss to the side of her throat.

My eyes turn to Evie, seeing she's watching me. With a little smirk on her lips, her eyes roam over my face. She lifts a brow. "See?"

I nod. "Okay, okay," I admit, "you were right. Nothing to worry about there."

"Told ya," she says with a wink behind her black lace mask, and I reach over and pinch her nipple through her robe and bra. She yelps then looks contrite, and I give her a devilish grin.

"Well, we're here, sweet Evie. Is there like... a room or somewhere we can go?" I ask, looking around at the curtained off alcoves on the other sides of the booths.

She shakes her head. "Not yet. You have to be certified first."

"Then where exactly do I get to enjoy my woman while we're here until that happens?" I prompt, and she gestures around the club with her wine glass before taking a sip.

"Anywhere out in the open," she replies, and I look around. Sure enough, there are people in all sorts of positions doing various sexual acts—inside the booths, up in the cages holding stripper poles, and right there on the dance floor. There are several people standing around and just watching, and somehow, they don't look like creepers. They come across more like spectators, learning from the acts in front of them. It's all voyeuristic and sensual, especially the couple beneath the two having sex in the cage, the man standing behind his woman, his arm wrapped around the front of her and his hand beneath her skirt as they watch. From the motion of his arm and the look on her face, he's finger-fucking her good, and soon, her knees buckle as she comes loudly.

I blow out a breath. "And when does my training start exactly?"

"Fridays are Seven's night off from training. But he has sessions all throughout the week and on Saturdays. I suppose Saturdays will be your night, since you'll already be on this side of town and probably won't be able to come during the school week," she explains, and I nod, leaning over to kiss her cheek. "You'll just have to make sure you don't wear me out too badly on Friday evenings."

I lift a brow. "And why is that?" I don't like the idea of being limited on what I get to do to her.

She stares me in the eyes with her lips slightly pinched. "Because during training, I will have to come with you, since you'll need a sub to practice his instructions on. And as jealous as you get over the idea of me being with any of these Doms in the past, I think you can understand quite clearly that I would not be okay with you using some other sub to train with."

Her spike of possessiveness makes my cock strain against my zipper, and before I even plan my attack, I snatch her wine glass out of her hand and shove it and my water out of the way. I grip her around the waist, and she squeals as I haul her up on top of the table before me. I take hold of her left thigh and pull her leg to the other side of me, placing her feet on the cushioned seat. I grip her knees in my big hands, watching her tits bounce as she jumps when it tickles. My eyes lift to hers.

"I can promise you, little mouse, you are the only submissive I will ever lay a hand on," I tell her, my voice deep and low.

She pouts out her bottom lip prettily. "There are other ways to dominate a sub without using your hands, Mr. Black," she murmurs, and I have to reach down to adjust my raging erection.

"Then I promise you, sweet Evie, you're my one and only. No part of me or object wielded by me will ever touch another woman but you, sub or otherwise," I clarify, and she reaches down and between her knees to cup my cheek.

"You asking me to go steady?" she asks, her voice overdramatically breathy as she smiles.

"Oh, I'm not asking, little mouse," I tell her, and I nip the inside of her thigh, making her squeak. "Now, lie back and hold still. Your Dom is suddenly *very* hungry."

And like the good little sub she is, she does exactly that.

EPILOGUE

Seven years later
    Evie

I pull at the straps holding my wrists hostage against the headboard, whimpering with need. He's been teasing me for... I don't even know how long. I've lost track of time. He's brought me to the brink of orgasm over and over again, and I both love and hate this new fetish he's suddenly been obsessed with, testing himself to see just how long he can stand *not* making me come. It's a competition I wish he'd go ahead and vote himself the winner for. That is, until he finally eventually lets me come, and it's so powerful I immediately fall headfirst into subspace.

But tonight feels like he's going for an all-time record, or maybe I'm just extra needy. I look down my body, covered in a tight-fitting white lace bodice that meets a skirt that flares at the waist like a big, poofy princess dress. At least, it did as I walked down the aisle toward him this afternoon, my hand gripping Doc's big bicep wrapped in a black tuxedo as he gave me away. For being such a big, tough man, it brought instant tears to my eyes the day I asked him if he'd be the one to give me away, and he'd gotten emotional, wiping a tear away and claiming there was dust in his eye.

Now though, the fluffy skirt was bunched up from my raised knees to my waist, looking like some kind of doctor's curtain, hiding what is going on between my thighs. So I have no way of knowing just what Nathaniel is going to do before he does it.

His fingers stroke inside me, swirling upward and rubbing at the secret spot inside me that makes my toes cramp I curl them so hard. My eyes roll back in my head before I sit my head up, feeling almost panicked I'm so... fucking... close. My breath comes out in pants and I look around the room that's starting to spin around me. Our special room designated to the D/s part of our relationship. It was the first room we decorated when we moved into our new house a year ago.

I whimper as he doesn't let up, and I pray—oh God do I pray—that this will finally be the time he lets me find release, and as he adds his thumb to my clit, I know... I know he's giving in. I throw my head back and scream as fireworks go off behind my eyes, climaxing so hard my entire existence stiffens and releases. And before I can fall under that mystical spell, he's above me, but all I can see is his tuxedo shirt and above, his bowtie hanging undone around his neck under the unbuttoned collar. And then my eyes nearly cross as I feel him enter me without warning, and he falls forward between my thighs, crushing the big skirt between us as his hands brace on either side of my head.

"Ready to consecrate this marriage, Mrs. Black?" he whispers, nuzzling his face into the side of my neck as he thrusts deep, bottoming out inside me.

"Yes!" I exhale, and he fucks into me hard.

"Yes, what?" he taunts, swirling his hips before pulling almost all the way out.

"Yes, Mr. Black," he allows me to say before he plunges back inside. "Oooh God," I moan as he works his cock just right to where it drags along my clit on the instroke, and my whole body shudders.

"Not going to last long this time, baby," he warns, and I am completely okay with that. It's been a really long day. "I've been wanting to get inside you since the moment those big doors opened and I got my first glimpse of you at the end of the aisle." He thrusts, nibbling along the top of my breast pushed up high from the corset bodice. "Never going another night without you, Evie. Last night was fucking bullshit," he says, and I let out an involuntary giggle.

He stops moving, pulling back to look down into my eyes. I look up at him deliriously, still tipsy from the champagne I drank at the reception, and most definitely drunk on him. "You think that's funny, little mouse?"

I smile up at him, taking in his lowered brows and flared nostrils, his sexy Dom face, but I know I don't have to worry too much, because as he said, he's wanted me far too much today and was forced to keep his hands off me while we were surrounded by his family and all our friends. "Just a little, Mr. Black."

He lifts a brow. "You provoking me?"

I shake my head languidly. "Nope, just here enjoying my husband's cock, thank you."

He groans, said cock twitching inside me. "Baby, fuck." He picks up his thrusts, closing his eyes for a moment and resting his forehead against mine. "Just so you know, I'm making a mental note to punish you for that later," he whispers. "But for now, I'm just going to enjoy my wife's tight…" Thrust. "…wet…" Thrust. "…pussy. Thank you."

I giggle, and he groans, swirling his hips, sitting back up and looking into my eyes. "You know your pussy squeezes me like a fist when you laugh?" he prompts, but all I can do is moan and blink at him as he reaches down between us, over the skirt, and finds my clit with two fingers. He pinches it gently, and my legs convulse, and he picks up his pace. "Something to explore later," he says absently, and then that's the end of all conversation, because he hikes his knees up higher beneath my hips, wraps his arm beneath my back to grasp my shoulder from behind to keep me anchored, and then he tosses the reins on his control to the wind, fucking me like it's our last time, when it's really our first as man and wife.

Several minutes later, when he's untied and undressed me and carried me out of our playroom and into our bedroom, he wraps me up in his arms after tucking the sheets around us. My head lays on his chest as he traces patterns along my back with his fingertips, lulling me to sleep. And in that moment just before I fall into oblivion, I feel him chuckle, hearing it deep inside his chest.

"What's so funny, Mr. Black?" I murmur, the words coming out mostly slurred.

"Oh, nothing, little mouse," he tells me low. "Just that I *black*mailed you into becoming Mrs. *Black*." He chuckles again.

I let out one exhausted, amused huff, and then I fall right to sleep.

The End

Dearest Reader,

Thank you for taking a chance on Nate! I'd love to have you in my reader group, KD-Rob's Mob. If you have a moment, please leave a review for *A Lesson in Blackmail*. Even if it's just one sentence on Amazon, it helps an author's work be seen by other readers. Goodreads and Bookbub are helpful too!

Love,
KD

Printed in Great Britain
by Amazon